Like Jaguar Eyes

A rom-com adventure set in the Brazilian Pantanal in the 1970s and 1980s.

By
Ellie Vivino

Contents

Prologue Jungle City, June 1985..1

Rio de Janeiro, 1977 Summer Sands and a Surprise Journey..3

Journey to Jungle City The Unexpected Surprises 8

The Return To Rio de Janeiro 16

Jungle City, 1980 A Seductive Deal 20

Heatwave and Hidden Treasure 25

Kitchen to Business...32

Sweaty Strolls and Sweet Moments......................................36

Jungle City, 1984 Rosettes..40

1984 - Journey to Dreams From Jungle to City Skies 47

A Rainy Encounter 51

The Jaguar's Gamble And Unravelling Charades 60

Double-Crossed Affairs And Whispers of Betrayal...............66

The Tour and the Longing..76

Departures and Discoveries...81

Strings of Fate 89

Flaky Candy and Second Chances...92

Unexpected Neighbors...96

The Slippery Scheme 101

The Attraction 104

A New Tour Gig 108

The Girl's Name 114

Sweet Encounters and Hidden Desires 117

Love, Loss, and Redemption in the Jungle 120

Emergency Response 122

A Rush Catering Drop-Off..126

An Unexpected Proposal..130

A Long-Awaited Reunion 135

The Unforeseen Bond.. 139

Pretenses... 142

The Search 147

The Rescue And The Jaguar... 150

Unintended Consequences 155

A Promise and New Beginnings 159

Shopping Spree 163

July 1985 - The World Watches... 166

Epilogue: Who's The Jaguar? Who's the Prey?.................... 169

ACKNOWLEDGMENTS.. 171

Had fun reading? 173

Explore more with the following thought-provoking questions for a more engaging experience. 173

What do you think? 173

Prologue

Jungle City, June 1985

With her versatile acting voice and animated performance, Mrs. Mae captivated her radio audience. "I believe Jaguars speak with their eyes. When laser-focused on their prey, their amber eyes seem to say, *I want you. You are mine.*

"But not the jaguar of today's story.

"As we know, the blazes burned through Jungle City. Volunteers wearing their signature Wildlife Rescuers shirts combed the burned area for wildlife survivors. After finding lifeless reptiles and capibaras, burned trees, and birds, they heard a faint roar. Advancing toward the sound, they saw it: the jaguar, defenseless and vulnerable in the sheltered shade beneath what remained of its Manduvi tree. Its paws were fire engine red, burned in the latest wildfire to sweep through the Pantanal. The jaguar opened its mouth but didn't move. And its gaze implored, *Help me.*

"Without hesitation, one of the volunteers took aim with a tranquilizer dart and nailed the shot. The jaguar gazed at the people around and closed its eyes. Another volunteer put a muzzle on the cat, and the team carefully lowered the animal to a stretcher. They brought the jaguar to the barn of Rancho Santa Fabiana for the veterinarian's assessment and further care. Stay tuned. The story continues after this word from our sponsors."

Meanwhile, in the barn, the injured jaguar lay on a gurney in a glass enclosure. Beyond the glass, volunteers watched as the vet inspected the jaguar's vulnerable crimson paws.

"Poor jaguar, it's as if you were walking barefoot on hot coals," Kathy, one of the rescuers, lamented, her eyes welling with tears. Glancing at her wristwatch, she looked around and spotted an old radio on a desk beside a sizable fan. She swiftly turned it on, selecting Mrs. Mae's show. Keeping an eye on the sedated jaguar and her ear attuned to the radio, Kathy expressed, "I love Mrs. Mae's saga series. Her style is so engaging. She puts us there in the middle of the scene." Kathy fine-tuned the volume, inviting everyone into the narrative.

At that moment, the opening music of the show filled the air. Mrs. Mae said on the radio microphone, "Good morning, esteemed listeners of *Narrative Waves Radio*, the station focused on delivering a variety of engaging and narrative-driven content. You are tuned into Mrs. Mae's *Words into Tangible Worlds*. I'm truly grateful for the warm welcome into your homes, workplaces, and wherever you may be on this hot and sunny day, as usual in Jungle City. Like a fly on the wall, I'm ready to embody many characters and to immerse myself in different minds. So, let our imagination take flight. Today, I bring you the intricate tale of ownership surrounding Rancho Santa Fabiana, a story that fatefully converges with our wounded jaguar."

After a brief special effect sound, Mrs. Mae began. "Let's go back in time. Eight years ago..."

Rio de Janeiro, 1977

Summer Sands and a Surprise Journey

On a windy day at Ipanema Beach in Rio de Janeiro, Fabiana and her friend Clara, both thirteen, were enjoying the warmth of the sun, watching their classmates play beach volleyball. The lithe and sun-kissed girls giggled while glancing at Fabiana's crush, Peter - a tanned teen in surf-themed swim trunks.

Manuelito, Fabiana's younger brother, was at Fabiana's feet, creating a sand castle. But the volleyball crushed it. Fabiana patted her brother's head and asked him to dig in the sand instead. Right then, Peter started walking toward her; she was delighted. Peter retrieved two tickets from his pocket and handed them to Clara, as he had promised earlier, without Fabiana's knowledge. Fabiana frowned, smoothed her T-shirt, and looked at Clara with a questioning expression. She sighed when Clara explained the tickets were for the musical that Peter's brother, her crush, was in.

Fabiana asked Peter if he would go to the theater, but Clara interrupted, saying her mom might let her go if Fabiana came too. She urged Fabiana to join her. Fabiana smiled at the boy.

Manuelito became impatient and said he wanted to go home for lunch. Fabiana and Clara waved to the teen, who was already back in the court. The girls took Manuelito's hands and crossed the busy street. They lived in a building as neighbors, with a peaking view of the Ipanema beach.

***

During lunch, Fabiana made a heartfelt request to her mother, pleading, "Mom, please let me go to the theater. Clara has two tickets. Her friend is in the play. She wants me to go with her." Pearl shook her head, but before she could take a bite of her salad, the telephone rang. Pearl answered and assured the caller that she would be there as soon as possible. As she hung up, Pearl's cheerful expression turned to one of concern as she sank back into her chair.

Fabiana was curious and asked, "Where are you going? Who was that on the phone?"

Pearl replied, "Dr. Machado. He says my father is very ill."

Stunned by this revelation, she asked, "Wait, what? You mean to say I have a grandpa? And he is alive? But you said he had died before I was born!"

Pearl explained, "It's complicated. Bottom line, he abandoned me."

Fabiana was eager to know more and asked, "What's his name and where is he now?"

"His name is Jackson and he's at home in Jungle City. I need to go there. You kids are coming along. I'm calling your dad and making reservations."

Manuelito was eager and said, "Cool! I'll take my camera and take lots of pictures of the wild animals."

Fabiana pouted. Going to Jungle City would mean leaving her crush behind and not going to the theater. She said she was scared of the wild animals that roam the jungle and didn't want to go. On the verge of tears, Fabiana retreated to her room, finding solace in her sketchbook. With a deep sigh, she sketched an eye, painting it crimson red as if it were on fire. In a burst of frustration, she exclaimed, "Mom, you must go by yourself."

Pearl ended the phone call with her husband and called out to Fabiana that they were leaving the next morning. Smoothing her T-shirt, the girl went back to the kitchen and said that she would only go if they traveled by plane. She then called Clara to tell her about her trip to Jungle City, which she described as being in the middle of nowhere.

The next day, Pearl's husband loaded their luggage into the car and drove them to Santos Dumont Airport. He couldn't come with them because of his work schedule.

Fabiana and her family boarded a VARIG Airlines plane headed for Campo Grande. After taking her assigned window seat, she later switched with Manuelito, who also wanted to see the view. Before landing, Fabiana asked the attendant if she could keep the onboard magazine, to which the attendant agreed.

Upon arrival at the Campo Grande airport, the family hailed a small Volkswagen taxi to reach the bus station.

***

Meanwhile, in Jungle City, the setting sun cast a golden light across the river full of aquatic plants. The jaguar had slept during the day and was now awake. He was draped around a sturdy branch of the Manduvi tree, one of the tallest trees in the Pantanal. Its hunger was growing. The jaguar surveyed the area with its amber eyes, searching for prey. Its rosette-patterned coat helped it blend in with the foliage of its territorial tree. Suddenly, the jaguar spotted a caiman resting motionless on the river bank with its mouth open. Right there and then, the jaguar had made up its mind. This was going to be the prey for today. With its eyes set on the caiman and paws ready to draw blood, the jaguar prepared itself. Not making any sudden movements, it waited and waited till the perfect opportunity came up. The caiman looked on the other side and that was the much-awaited distraction the predator needed. And then, the jaguar pounced.

***

Glorieta, a woman with brown eyes enhanced by heavy mascara, watched over the sick man. She had agreed to care for him two weeks earlier, assuming he had no relatives.

Just yesterday, she had mentioned her upcoming thirty-fifth birthday, which was a lie. The sick man nodded. Encouraged, Glorieta suggested he give her his dilapidated ranch. He nodded again. She added she didn't mind that the main house had burned down years ago. The movement of the ceiling fan made the man drowsy, and he tried to drift off into a nap. Glorieta interpreted his nodding while falling asleep as consent.

This morning, she entered the room dancing to her own version of a cha-cha-cha. She tapped his hands and sang, "You will sign the deed when you wake up." She had a smile on her face as she left the room. Sitting herself in the living room, she grabbed a magazine and started reading and soon started daydreaming.

She thought of her last rendezvous. It was two weeks ago. Carrying a box of chocolate, Monlevade arrived as he usually did at Glorieta's house without prior announcement. Wasting no time while Ceeda, her maid, greeted him at the door, Glorieta went to the kitchen to get the glass container of sugar. After bringing it to her bedroom and leaving it on her night-table, she entered the living room, welcomed Monlevade, and asked Ceeda to serve coffee. A few minutes later, the maid returned to apologize for the lack of sugar.

"Go buy it. You know I hate to drink coffee without sugar." Glorieta winked at Monlevade, who chuckled.

As soon as Ceeda left, Monlevade said, "My sugar." Pressing her against the wall, he walked toward her bedroom. She took the chocolate box from him, but he took it back and threw it towards the night-table. The box knocked the container of sugar onto the tiled floor. The glass broke, splashing its content. Glorieta rolled her eyes, looked at her wristwatch, and said, "Max of 15 minutes."

She kept her eyes wide open as Monlevade started kissing her neck and unbuttoned her silk shirt to bury his face on her plump chest. Glorieta endured his passionate, slobbery, grunting passion for as long as she could stand, then grabbed his head and said, "Let's talk about Rancho Santa Fabiana."

"Yah, my sugar. Let's transform it into 'Resort Santa Glorieta.' We just need the signed deed of the land. I'll take care of the rest."

"Perfect! You can go right ahead. For now, wipe that cute smirk off your face, and let's go to the living room. Ceeda will be back at any minute."

Glorieta was used to Monlevade disappearing for long periods, returning unannounced to whisper in her ears, *My sugar, I'll take care of you.*

Journey to Jungle City

The Unexpected Surprises

After a long six-hour bus ride on bumpy roads, Pearl, Fabiana, and Manuelito arrived in Jungle City feeling exhausted. As they stumbled out of the bus, a shirtless man carrying a Styrofoam box approached them with cups of cold water. Pearl bought three cups, and they all drank as if they were in the Sahara desert.

Fabiana complained about the brutal and bouncing bus ride, and Pearl nodded in agreement. The scorching heat made Fabiana's forehead sweat. She called attention to the street thermometer on the median, which showed 104 degrees Fahrenheit. Pearl was also sweating and asked Fabiana for a tissue. Fabiana gave her a magazine from her bag, and Pearl used it as a fan. Pearl suggested taking a cab to her father's house, which was only ten minutes away, but the heat made it unbearable to walk.

***

As Manuelito got out of the cab, he lifted his camera toward the sky. "Look at that!" he exclaimed, seeing the blue macaws flying over the small brick house. "And listen to those loud crickets. Wow!"

"I thought it would be a bigger house," Fabiana commented. "Where will we sleep? Is there even a bathroom?"

"It's actually bigger than it looks. It has three bedrooms and a very nice bathroom," Pearl replied. "I grew up in this house and always enjoyed watching toucans and jabirus..."

"Jabirus?" Manuelito asked.

"Yes, we call them tuiuiú."

"To-you-you? Cool," Manuelito said as he took pictures of everything around him.

Pearl carried her suitcase to the door and knocked. The woman answered the door, giving them a suspicious look.

"I'm Jackson's daughter," Pearl explained.

"Glorieta, the caregiver," the woman grudgingly replied. "He told me he didn't have any living relatives."

Pearl flushed. "Dr. Machado called me. He said I should come. These are my kids, his grandchildren."

"Please wait here," Glorieta told Pearl before shutting the door. In the sick man's room, she shook him up and woke him. With a shrieking voice, she asked, "Jackson, Jackson, please tell me you don't have a daughter." He confirmed he did, though he seemed a bit disoriented. "Has she arrived yet?" he asked. Glorieta nodded and walked away. She paced back and forth in the living room for about five minutes, not knowing what to do, her arms crossed and lips pressed. Eventually, she opened the front door, letting Pearl and her children come in. Glorieta remained muted as they entered.

Pearl said she knew her way around and went to her father's bedroom with Glorieta and the children in tow. With tearful eyes, Jackson held his estranged daughter's hand. He then asked Glorieta to leave them alone for a moment. She rolled her eyes but left the room. Just before she shut the door, he added, "Fix us some breakfast, too." Glorieta let out a big sigh and walked away.

Pearl introduced her children to their grandfather. Unsure of how to respond to the man who had given her an ultimatum - her husband or her home - she excused herself and expressed the need to take a shower. She carried her luggage into her childhood bedroom. Looking around, she searched through her drawers and closets, only to find them empty of all her belongings. Nothing remained to evoke her memories there. Sighing, she reached for the suitcase to take out fresh clothes. Then she moved on to the bathroom.

As soon as Glorieta heard the shower, she pressed her ear against Jackson's bedroom door and heard him coughing. His cough was loud and concerning.

Jackson asked Fabiana to collect two boxes and a manila envelope from the top of his dresser. Opening a box, he said, "You'll need this in the jungle. A machine to tranquilize animals." Manuelito held it in his hand. "It'll only sedate the animal. After that, get the hell out of there as fast as possible," Jackson said.

Fabiana was hesitant. The machine looked like a gun with a place for a syringe. "I don't think we will stay long enough to come across wild creatures." But he insisted, asking her to take the tranquilizer gun, and she did.

Glorieta rolled her eyes and muttered under her breath. "Stupid kids, I hope you come face to face with a man-eating jaguar. We'll see how well your stupid grandpa's suggestions work."

The sound of the bathroom door being opened forced Glorieta to move into the kitchen in order to avoid being caught eavesdropping. Pearl entered her dad's room in time to hear him ask, "Manuelito, you are what, seven years old? I'll give your box to your mom for safekeeping."

He handed the box to his daughter and continued, "And Pearl, this envelope is for you."

She opened it and took out a letter she had sent him to announce Fabiana's birth.

Glorieta sidled back up to Jackson's bedroom door.

"Pearl, I named the ranch after Fabiana. This is the first and the only one of your letters I kept. All the others I sent back in fury without reading. At least I learned the name of my granddaughter." He turned to face Fabiana. "I'm leaving my ranch to you, young lady. Do not, under any circumstance," he coughed loudly, "tell ... 'bout it before you get married." Then he was short of breath and convulsing.

Loud trucks outside the window muffled Jackson's words.

Old bastard! Did I hear that right? You said the girl can only sell after she gets married? Rancho Santa Fabiana should be mine. I have plans for this place. It will be mine. Mine! Glorieta mumbled to herself and rushed back to the kitchen when she heard someone approaching the door.

Fabiana found Glorieta preparing a tray with jello, juice, and crackers. "Miss, you must call a priest! Hurry!" The girl asked and rushed back to her grandfather's side.

"Who do you think you are to boss me around, you brat?" Glorieta thought to herself before glancing at the phone book on the corner table in the living room. She flipped its pages, almost tearing them. Then she took a moment to collect herself and reentered the bedroom. She called Fabiana aside and handed her a piece of paper. "I tried to call the church secretary, and there was no answer," she lied. "Here is the address of the church. It's near the high school. Go there and ask a priest to come. I cannot run or walk as quickly as you." Glorieta put her arm around Fabiana's shoulders and walked her towards the front door.

Fabiana removed herself from Glorieta's gripping hands and returned to the bedroom. She grabbed her tote bag, placed the tranquilizing machine inside it, and headed outside.

***

Johnny was looking forward to eating the mashed potatoes that his mother's maid, Ceeda, was preparing for his fifteenth birthday. However, he had to give a forged note from his mother to his P.E. teacher explaining that he had a doctor's appointment. The substitute teacher looked at Johnny and then put the note in his pocket. Johnny was nervous and stared back at the teacher, but he gestured for him to leave and blew his whistle to gather the rest of the students.

Johnny punched the air after leaving the school grounds. After all, it was his birthday; why should he have to spend his special day doing exhausting exercises and being mocked for having a bit of extra weight? Unbeknownst to him, two of his classmates were following him as they skipped the same class. When they reached an isolated street corner, the two skinny kids pushed Johnny onto the pavement. They called him offensive names and then threw him against the brick wall. Johnny knelt down and covered his head with his arms.

Fabiana turned the corner and froze when she saw the boys fighting. Not wanting to get involved in the altercation, she crossed the street.

Johnny's bullies grabbed his books from his backpack and tossed them up in the air for the sole purpose of entertaining themselves. One of the books hit Fabiana in the head, and she massaged the spot. One of the bullies noticed Fabiana as she opened her tote bag and, in a split second, took out the unloaded tranquilizer gun. Shaking, she walked toward the scene.

The bullies looked at the tall teenager threatening them and asked her to take it easy. They said they were helping the poor boy off the ground and pulled Johnny back on his feet just to prove it. But Johnny shoved their hand away and kept his arms over his head. The boys patted Johnny's head and scattered away in two different directions.

Fabiana felt sick to her stomach. She stuffed the gun back into her bag, her mind racing with terrifying images. *"What if I had found a jaguar attacking this poor kid? No, Jungle City is definitely not for me."* She shook her head and collected Johnny's books before approaching him.

She tapped his shoulder and said the bullies had gone. As he opened his eyes, the sun was peeking through the clouds. To his amazement, in front of him stood a heavenly figure who he thought was an angel. His eyes hovered over the words *I Love Rio* on the angel's t-shirt.

"Your nose is bleeding," the angel pointed out.

Johnny placed his thumb over his nostril to halt the flow of blood.

"I'm sorry, but I'm in a hurry. I'm searching for a priest."

"The church is around that corner - right over there."

"Thanks," the angel replied and left.

Johnny got up. Speechless, he watched the "angel" disappear down the street corner.

***

Pearl clasped her father's thin fingers. "I'm so sorry, Dad. For all the time we've missed."

Jackson replied, "I blame myself. Not your fault, dear. Is Bobby … a good husband?"

"The best. He's great with the kids and me."

"Then that's all that matters. Sorry for everything. I know it's all my fault. I should have let you marry him. I thought Bobby was a gold digger. I couldn't see past the fact that he was my maid's son. I was wrong and unreasonable. I never should have sent you away," he said with teary eyes.

Glorieta brought Fabiana and the priest into the bedroom and left the room. Pearl thanked the priest for coming. While the priest began setting up his holy water, Jackson turned to Pearl. "I want…," he coughed, "you… to take a message… to Campo Grande on your way home... Madame Sophia… Her address is in my Rolodex."

"Of course." Pearl choked back a sob. "What do you want me to tell her?"

"Ask her to forget about…," Jackson gasped for air.

"Dad, forget about what?"

Pearl held her children. The old man's eyes were open, but he no longer saw them.

Under the tearful eyes of Pearl and the kids, the priest approached and administered the last rites.

***

In the kitchen, Glorieta absentmindedly poured water into a glass, unaware that it was spilling over the rim. Her eyes shot daggers with the intensity of a jaguar ready to pounce. Her body tensed as she foresaw her plans with Monlevade evaporate in thin air.

Back in Jackson's bedroom, she felt nothing but derision when Pearl closed her father's eyes. Assuring the family they had nothing to worry about, Glorieta added she would make the announcement to Jackson's friends. Shaking her head, she backed out of the bedroom and left the house without a word. She stopped at a coffee shop and told the owner to send his customers to the cemetery. Glorieta never returned to Jackson's house to help Pearl clean up but sent a sympathy card with instructions for the family to send her paycheck.

***

The funeral took place the following day. Pearl thanked the poor and tired people who, she later learned, had worked for Jackson a few years back, gathered at the cemetery on that rainy afternoon.

"Mom." Fabiana said, "I hope you were able to make peace with Grandpa."

"Why was Grandpa apologizing?" Manuelito asked.

Pearl hugged her children. "My father's short temper closed many doors. He was furious when I married your father and kicked us out of his life. He returned all my letters unopened. But he was sorry for all the lost time, and he truly loved meeting both of you."

With the kid's help, Pearl sorted her late father's belongings. Since the kids had no use for the tranquilizer guns in Rio, she put them in a drawer in the kitchen.

Manuelito found three fans in the barn and carried them into the house to combat the intense heat of Jungle City. Pearl found her mother's old blender. It still worked. She made fresh watermelon juice, and the kids gulped it down.

Two weeks later, they packed and walked to the bus station. While waiting for the overnight bus, Pearl sobbed. Fabiana and Manuelito put their arms around her shoulders. Their tears mixed.

"Grandpa didn't need to leave me anything," Fabiana said. "But I'm glad you said goodbye to him."

The Return To Rio de Janeiro

Manuelito slept during the bumpy overnight bus ride back to Campo Grande. Upon arriving, the family had to wait until the evening to board their flight to Rio de Janeiro. Fanning themselves with magazines, they entered the next cab approaching the queue, and Pearl gave the address to the driver. After a fifteen-minute ride, the cab stopped in front of a small house covered in ivy.

Madame Sophia, a woman in her sixties, had her long hair pulled up in a bun. She pushed her oversized Sophia Loren glasses up the bridge of her nose and looked through the window to see who was knocking at her door. Pearl introduced herself and explained that her late father had sent her there.

"Who?"

"Jackson, the owner of Rancho Santa Fabiana. His last words were," Pearl stopped for a second, "ask Sophia to forget about it."

"Forget about it? Oh, dear. I'm so sorry for your loss, but it's been such a long time. I have forgotten it, whatever it may be, already." Madame Sophia chuckled.

She invited the family in, offered coffee with crackers, and offered Fabiana a manicure with a design of her choice. Fabiana's face lit up but soon faded as Sophia continued, "When you come back to Jungle City." She smiled. "Until then, let me read the future. I can be a fortune reader."

Motioning for the girl to sit at a table displaying a deck of playing cards and a vintage turban, she winked and skillfully positioned the faded headpiece on her head.

Fabiana seemed excited as she quickly got ready.

"Let's see what's in store for you. Cut this deck in three piles and place them face-down." Fabiana obliged.

Madame Sophia turned the first card up and said, "The present. You like traveling, heh? I know you are traveling, but this could be today's trip or a future trip by plane."

Turning the middle card up, Madame Sophia said, "The past. An admirer. There's someone waiting for you, but I'm not sure where."

"And finally, the future. Disentanglement. Aha! Good things are coming your way, but you must go over some unfinished business."

"Could that be a concert?"

"It could be. But I sense it's something else." Madame Sophia sighed. She removed her turban, collected the cards, and stored them in the box.

Madame Sophia kept winking at Pearl, who suppressed a smile as Fabiana was surprised by the quickness of the reading.

A few hours later, after exchanging heartfelt goodbyes with Madame Sophia, the family headed to the airport. Brimming with anticipation, Fabiana could hardly wait to the flight back home.

***

Bobby picked the family up in Rio de Janeiro. He kissed his wife and hugged his children.

"Dad apologized for the way he treated you before he died, hon." Pearl watched her husband's face for some type of reaction. He was furious with the chaotic traffic leading to Ipanema Beach. "He left the ranch to Fabiana. But he told her she can't sell it." Pearl sighed, "Do you think we have the means to manage it from here?"

Bobby shook his head. The street light turned green, and he honked his horn. The car in front had to keep moving.

"Daddy, I don't want to live in Jungle City," Fabiana complained.

Bobby nodded, smiled, and asked the kids a few questions about their trip. Manuelito said it was really cool and he couldn't wait to work on developing his film. Fabiana rolled her eyes and said that she would never leave Rio to live in the middle of nowhere.

***

Glorieta was reclining in her bed at home. It was a dark house with two bedrooms. In the room where she sat, a monochromatic tube TV rested on top of her dresser across from her bed, and a black rotary telephone was on top of her night table. Glorieta always kept a box of chocolate in the nightstand drawer.

In Johnny's bedroom, a poster of Botticelli's Birth of Venus adorned the wall. Unfortunately, there was no garage and Glorieta never found parking in front of her house. In her bedroom and in the living room, dark curtains covered the windows that look out onto the street.

The phone rang in Glorieta's room and she picked up while enjoying a bonbon. She listened and stated, "Thank you for remembering my birthday. And, yes, dear, you can mark my words. Rancho Santa Fabiana will be mine." She shrugged and moved the phone from her ear as the caller's voice escalated in volume. Mellowing, she said, "Of course, that's what I meant. If everything goes according to the plans, we'll share it. One day, it will be my birthday gift." Glorieta slammed the phone on the receiver and annoyed, rolled her eyes.

Over the next few days, Glorieta added more coats of mascara to her eyes. She vented her frustrations onto her maid, Ceeda, her teenage son, Johnny, and her former husband, Joao. She cursed Jackson and called him 'the deceased hermit.' "He wasn't supposed to have any family. He led me to believe the ranch would be my birthday gift. No way in hell I'm going to let that brat have my land. I'm going to get that deed and together with Monlevade, we turn that ranch into a resort and make a fortune."

Glorieta propped herself up in bed and consumed several chocolates from the box on her lap. Johnny came to her open door with a permission form for a school retreat. He asked if he could have some of her candy. "Go look at yourself in the mirror," she screamed. "You are going to turn into an elephant!"

Johnny sighed, left the doorway, went to his bedroom, and forged his mother's signature once again. Then, staring at the ceiling, he invoked, "Angel! Angel!"

Jungle City, 1980

A Seductive Deal

Glorieta rose from the bed, selected a front-button dress, and pinned an oversized silk camellia to the waistband. She combed her short hair and applied a cheap citrusy perfume. Then she went to the only bank in Jungle City and demanded to see Vice President Prestle.

Prestle, a septuagenarian with a mischievous grin on his round face, rose to greet her with a handshake. The intercom light lit and the receptionist said, "Your ex-wife is on line two." Prestle ignored it and turned his attention to Glorieta. The receptionist peeked inside the room and said, "Sorry, Mr. Prestle. Your ex-wife said it's urgent. She is now on line three." Prestle asked Glorieta for a moment.

Glorieta turned her back to him and looked at the pictures on the wall. When she heard him whispering, "We are through," she raised her eyebrows and discreetly unbuttoned one button from the top and one from the bottom of her dress.

Prestle hung up the phone, shaking his head. Composing himself, he invited Glorieta to sit down.

With an air of indifference, she chose a comfy armchair by the window. She lifted her torso, puffing her ample cleavage, and crossed her legs. Though Prestle was in his late seventies, at least thirty years her senior, Glorieta was delighted to see him staring at her pushed-together breasts. After the initial greetings, she said she wanted to talk about a particular piece of real estate. She warned Prestle he would soon receive a visit from an investor named Monlevade, the owner of Sandy Lagoons.

Prestle offered her coffee.

She leaned forward to show more of her cleavage. "Anything stronger on offer?"

"Whisky! Would you like it?"

"Absolutely," she replied.

Prestle walked across the room to the credenza. He took off his reading glasses and opened the cabinet.

Glorieta got up and moved behind him. When he turned to hand her the drink, his face was at the same height as her chest. He chuckled. They clicked their glasses of whisky and cheered, "To a rewarding relationship."

After refilling their glasses a couple more times, she winked at him. Glorieta pointed to the door, and Prestle locked it. Her manicured fingers enticed him to get closer when he turned back to her. He moved toward her and stood in front of her, sniffing the cheap perfume emanating from her cleavage. From that day on, they would meet secretly in his office for their secret rendezvous.

One day, Glorieta purred into Prestle's ears, causing him to beam with delight. Seizing the moment, she requested that he make an advisory position for her in the bank. He answered, "Let me think about it, my Glo."

After a few glasses of whisky, Glorieta touched the base of his neck with her long fingernails and combed his hair upwards. He squealed with delight. "Prestle, my dear, there are two things I do exceptionally well – lunch and shopping. I can take your important clients to lunch and I can shop for clothes that you'd like me to wear. Wouldn't that be good?"

Prestle liked the idea and mentioned he had a bit of a fetish for sexy, laced bras. "You pervert," she teased. Laughing at his puzzled face, she purred and said, "I love it."

Glorieta began receiving a monthly stipend from Prestle and was listed as an advisor in the bank's accounts. She ditched her little car and traded it for the allure of a Mercedes leased by the bank.

She indulged in designer outfits, accessories, shoes, and perfume, telling Prestle it was all part of the bank rep style. Unbeknownst to Prestle, she skimped on business lunches, ordering inexpensive items for the clients and shifting the rest of the money to her personal account. Afterward, she would always return to the bank and model her latest bra for Prestle, letting him bury his nose in her scented cleavage.

A few months later, Glorieta asked Prestle to give her then eighteen-year-old son Johnny a job as a teller. It wasn't long before Prestle rewarded Glorieta's services to the bank by promoting Johnny to a manager, giving him his own office with a window.

***

Meanwhile, in Rio de Janeiro, Fabiana's father worked for an accounting company. At the end of the year, the office closed early to celebrate the Secret Santa potluck party. The employees exchanged gifts and imbibed various beverages. At seven, Bobby glanced at his watch and left the office in a hurry.

He shared his birthdate with Pearl, and the family was waiting for him to celebrate with a cake decorated by his children.

Fabiana placed a candle numbered 35 for Pearl, while Manuelito placed 36 for Bobby on each side of the rectangular cake, respectively.

It was a heavy rainy night with lightning and thunder.

The windshield wipers in Bobby's old VW car were worn out, and he squinted his eyes to see through the rain. The beams of the oncoming headlights and the rain pounding against his windshield obscured his view. He crashed into a Fiat driven by a newlywed woman. They both died on impact.

It was almost midnight. Pearl convinced her children that their father was working late and asked them to go to bed. They pouted but obeyed.

Pearl spent the night crying and worrying that her husband was leaving them. In the morning, she called her husband's office and spoke with his secretary, who said he was not in his office.

A few hours later, the police knocked at Pearl's door. They asked her to accompany them to the morgue. As she realized who was lying on the table, she sobbed aloud. With a shaky voice, she confirmed the deceased man was her husband. With tears rolling down her face, she delivered the bad news to her children. They hugged and cried together.

Bobby's entire office offered condolences and attended the funeral.

***

A few months later, the deceased newlywed's husband sued Bobby's estate. The court found Bobby liable for the accident. As a result, their apartment, furniture, and car were auctioned to pay their legal fees, judgment, and debts.

Save for an education trust in the kids' names, Pearl, a homemaker her entire life, found herself destitute with no source of income. After several sleepless nights, she came across her late father's deed to Rancho Santa Fabiana.

It was during dinner one night that she informed Fabiana and Manuelito that they were going to return to Jungle City.

Fabiana stomped her feet and said she would prefer to live with Clara than to go back to what she considered the middle of nowhere.

Pearl reminded her they had a house in Jungle City, and Fabiana had Rancho Santa Fabiana. Both places direly needed some loving, tender care.

Manuelito was excited because he loved photography and relished the opportunities to take wildlife pictures there. He also asked Pearl for a Polaroid camera.

"Why?" intervened Fabiana.

"That way, I can see the pictures developed right away."

Fabiana asked Pearl to give him the Polaroid only if he would take pictures of her.

Manuelito wasn't open to Fabiana's idea but was eager to receive the camera. "Of course. I'll set a few rules and take pictures of you. Yeah! With pleasure, sis!"

***

One year after the tragic car accident, Fabiana said goodbye to Clara, "I can't believe I'm going to live in the middle of nowhere. I promise to come back and visit you."

Fabiana was excited to travel by plane again but was not looking forward to the six-hour bus trip on unpaved roads right after that. Clutching his camera, Manuelito raced for the window seat in both the airplane and bus. "In case the glowing eyes of a jaguar peer out from the dense jungle," he teased his sister. However, the bumpy road soon lulled him to a deep sleep.

Heatwave and Hidden Treasure

The bus entered Jungle City and passed by the large thermometer placed on Main Street. Seventeen-year-old Fabiana looked at it and complained, "104 again? Is this for real?" She wiped away the sweat from her forehead.

"Don't do that," Manuelito warned. "Let it evaporate."

The humidity had turned Fabiana's short hair frizzy and curly. "Argh! Is there even a decent parlor in this place!" She frowned and glanced around the rundown Mom and Pop stores of the area.

The family settled in Pearl's childhood house. There were two small barns in the backyard. Fabiana chose the taller one and said she would transform it into an art studio. Pearl put a shelf on the back porch and started experimenting with seeds. She put sweet potatoes suspended by toothpicks in plastic containers with water and waited for the roots to sprout.

Eleven-year-old Manuelito explored the small barn and came across a twenty-six-inch men's single-speed charcoal *Caloi* bicycle with a torn leather saddle covered in duct tape and a rusty back seat. It was perfect for his five feet in height. He also came across an old Pentax camera. Pearl confirmed that the bike and the camera had belonged to her late father. After school, Manuelito shopped for a new saddle, kickstand, tires, and rust cleaners. He enjoyed working on restoring the bike.

On one of the 100-degree days, Manuelito gathered his mom and sister in the backyard. Like a magician, he slowly removed the waterproof cover from his bike. Pearl and Fabiana congratulated the proud boy.

"Wait, the surprise isn't over yet," he said, removing the cover from the handlebars.

Pearl clapped with delight and said, "The front basket is perfect. I love it."

"Even the bottles sweat here," Fabiana said, looking at the cold soft-drink bottles in the front basket.

Manuelito shrugged and offered them the drinks. "I just took them out of the fridge five minutes ago. Look at the sweat as vapor, sis." They fanned themselves and gulped the lukewarm beverage under the canopy of a mango tree.

***

One afternoon, Manuelito came home with a Kodak roll of film bought at the small drugstore. He inserted the roll in the Pentax, strapped the camera across his torso, and wrote a note that was left on the dining table: "Riding my bike. Be right back."

Standing by the door of her studio, Fabiana watched as her brother climbed his shining bike. She asked him where he was going.

"To your ranch. Wanna come along?"

Fabiana shook her head.

"In that case, *tchau*," he waved goodbye and started pedaling.

"No, wait. I'll come with you," Fabiana yelled as she ran after him and eventually hopped on the back of the bike. "Do you have your tranquilizer gun?"

"Not only that, but also a nature guidebook."

They stopped on the way to take pictures of flamboyant pink trumpet trees and the toucans they found perched on palm trees.

When they reached the ranch's entrance, they climbed off the bike, stretched their cramped muscles, and took in the panoramic view.

Manuelito started the conversation, "I don't know why you don't like it here, sis. I think it's a paradise."

"Yeah! The Pink Jacaranda tree is nice. But see those tall trees in the distance? The leafless ones? They look run down," Fabiana said.

Manuelito perused his book. "The Tabebuia trees. Wow! Look! A nest. I wonder what bird made it," Manuelito held his camera and zoomed in on a Tabebuia tree.

"That big bunch of dried twigs?" Fabiana pointed to the other side of the river. "That nest in that tree looks like it's in ruins, just like this ranch."

"Do you want to know or not?"

"Know what?"

"The bird that built the nest."

"I know. It's called Tuiuiu, Mr. Know-it-all."

"Well, the real name is Jabiru. Anyway, this place is fantastic," Manuelito said.

"Grampa should have sold it. This place requires lots of maintenance and money, which we don't have."

"In any case, I think you could design a better sign to replace that one." He pointed to the sign that read: PRIV---- P--PERTY --- TRESPASSIN-.

"Hop on, let's keep going." Manuelito climbed on the bike. As soon as Fabiana put her arms around his waist, the young boy started pedaling. "Let's look for jaguars." He did his impression of a jaguar roar.

"Stop that!" Fabiana hit him lightly in the arm. "Your pathetic meow might attract one."

"And what you are wearing won't? Snakeskin boots? Alligator top?" he joked.

"They are rosettes. Jaguar rosette pattern. Not alligator, you goofball. But, seriously, I'm afraid of snakes and caimans and jaguars…"

"You worry too much, sis. Snakes can't pierce your boots. But they may get angry when they recognize your snakeskin boots and hiss at you." Manuelito laughed out loud. "And if you see a jaguar, make yourself look big. That's what Grandpa told me."

They rode on the road covered with pebbles that crunched under the tires of the bike. Manuelito spotted the side of a dilapidated barn peeking through the dense jungle. He leaned the bike against a palm tree and pulled the heavy scrub forest sideways with their hands.

Something rattled the foliage to their left. "Get the tranquilizing gun," Fabiana said. Then she saw the flash of white storks and relaxed slightly. "It's just birds."

"Follow me." Manuelito took a few steps into the jungle and Fabiana followed, scanning their surroundings.

A couple of feet away, Manuelito said, "Look, an old barn by the river. It looks like it's burnt. Wanna see it?"

"No," Fabiana pulled on his shirt. "I think we should go back. We've come too far. Let's not take any risks."

Unbeknownst to them, at that moment, a caiman crawled from the right side of the barn into the bushes.

"Okay. The last one to reach the bike will walk home." Manuelito sprinted back to the bike and started down the road.

Fabiana ran behind, begging him to wait for her.

Manuelito finally slowed near the ranch's entrance. "Hop on and hold tight. I'm going to fly. Come on! Fast! I need to go to the bathroom."

Trying to catch her breath, Fabiana took her seat. "Never do that again."

The minute they got home, she jumped off the bike and ran into the house. "Something smells good in here," she said to Pearl before dashing down the hall to the bathroom and locking the door.

Manuelito parked the bike in the backyard, entered, and asked, "Mom? Is dinner ready? I'm starving," and ran to the bathroom. Skipping on his feet, he knocked several times, pleading, "Come on, sis. I'm sorry, very sorry. I really need to use the bathroom."

"Go outside," Fabiana yelled, studying her face in the mirror. A few minutes later, figuring Manuelito had learned his lesson, she finally relented and went to join her mother at the dining table.

Manuelito joined them, flicking water from his wet hands on Fabiana before he sat down.

"Thanks," Fabiana said, "That's… refreshing."

"I'm hungry, Mom."

Pearl served a slice of the freshly baked heart-of-palm pie to each and watched them eat.

"Delicious, I really like it," Fabiana said.

"I'm still hungry. More, please," Manuelito brought his plate forward while gulping the last spoonful.

"Mom, we saw the barn," Fabiana said and also brought her plate forward for another serving.

"Which barn? Oh! Don't tell me you went to the ranch."

"Yes," Fabiana said. "It's my property, isn't it? Why the surprise?"

"Was there a fire there?" Manuelito asked.

"Yes. It happened in 1972. We were living in Rio. You were a toddler, Manuelito. I heard about it on the radio and immediately phoned my Dad. But he never answered. I called the next-door rancher, the hospital, and the fire department, and spoke with the Chief who said he spoke with my father and relayed that Dad had big plans to rebuild the ranch. I can only guess Dad didn't have the strength to follow up. He also mentioned that Dad had moved into town to this very house and had a live-in assistant."

"I remember her being here when we came to visit Grandpa," Fabiana said.

"No, darling. I never knew who the lady was, but I heard she was an older woman. But speaking of Glorieta, I reconnected with her."

"Why, Mom? She was so cold to us when grandpa died," Fabiana said.

"Well, I grew up here. After I got married and moved to Rio – Well, no one I knew back then lives here anymore."

"But Mom, she is so creepy. Why do you need her?" Fabiana said.

"Yes, weirdo Glorieta," Manuelito added.

"Kids, no name-calling, please. I opened a business account and applied for a credit line. Glorieta called to welcome me to the bank and to say my father was so nice to her. I told her about my catering business and she said she can set me up with some clients."

"Any dessert?" Manuelito broke the silence that ensued.

"Sure. My passion-fruit mousse."

Pearl gave each a form that had four columns: description, how to improve, tasting grade, and comments, as well as several empty rows. Tonight's row was about the heart-of-palm pie and the passion-fruit mousse.

"Please complete it, okay? I know you liked it, but please let me know if there's anything that I can do to make my recipe better."

Under the 'How to Improve' column, Manuelito wrote, 'take pictures,' and Fabiana suggested some 'markers with the name of the pie and the mousse.' She assured Pearl that she would think of a way to design them. As for the grade, both gave it an eight for the heart-of-palm pie. Fabiana commented that the dough was too heavy because of the area's climate. Manuelito said it was a little too salty. As for the passion fruit mousse, it got a ten. It was light and refreshing.

Over the following days and nights, Pearl served new recipes, and Fabiana and Manuelito filled the rows. Cupcakes, grade ten. Onion pie, grade seven - good, but too heavy for the jungle's heat. Suggestion: smaller pies. Pineapple mousse, grade ten. When Pearl settled in bed every night, she rejoiced in reading the forms completed by her children.

***

Even though it was not a leap year, on the last day of February 1982, Pearl and Manuelito surprised Fabiana with a birthday cake. "Happy eighteenth birthday, dear daughter."

"Yeah! Congrats, sis. I'll take your picture when I get my Polaroid."

"But you have Grandpa's Pentax."

"That's for photos of nature. Besides, I know you'd wanna see your picture right away. As you know, my birthday is around the corner, and there are two things I'd like to get. A ticket to Rock in Rio and a Polaroid camera."

"You wish," Fabiana teased.

Pearl laughed at the siblings' exchange, shook her head, and left for her bedroom to read her mail. She opened the envelope from Jungle City Bank and excitedly said, "Finally!"

Kitchen to Business

In the following month, Pearl caught Glorieta off guard when she called to announce that the bank loan she had applied for had been approved. Thanks to the credit line from Jungle City Bank, she was finally able to start her business. She rented a four-room stucco house on Main Street, turning one of the bedrooms into her office, and fixing up the kitchen.

Rolling her eyes on the other side of the line, Glorieta asked if Pearl was going to add the latest, must-have appliance – the microwave. Pearl said that she could not afford it nor a dishwasher, but Lourdes, her helper, didn't mind washing everything by hand. "Actually, Lourdes has a strange obsession with washing the floor with soap and water," Pearl confided to Glorieta before ending the call with a chuckle.

Glorieta slammed the phone down and grabbed a box of chocolate, devouring the entire package in a few minutes, "Pearl, don't you expect me to take you out for lunch! That won't happen."

The last thing Glorieta wanted was a welcome luncheon for Pearl. Finger-combing Prestle's hair and implying Pearl's inability to repay the loan, she suggested that Prestle order lunch for the employees instead.

***

Fabiana and Manuelito went to the bank to drop off the catering order. Manuelito waited outside under the canopy of a tree while Fabiana brought the food inside and placed it at the reception desk. Twenty-year-old Johnny walked past her and could hardly believe his eyes as he saw Fabiana's T-shirt with the words *I Love Rio* printed across it.

Johnny smiled charmingly and asked, "Have we met before? I will never forget a face." He waited for Fabiana's reaction. "It's me, the guy from school. You saved me from bullies five years ago? Do you remember me?"

Fabiana studied Johnny's stubbled face. It contrasted with the image of the young teenager in fear.

"You were looking for a priest. You were wearing an I *Love Rio* T-shirt." He looked excited.

"No way! You, that boy? How are you? What are you doing here? Do you work here?"

"Yes, as a manager. I'm Johnny, by the way."

"Pleased to meet again, Mr. Johnny, by the way," she said with a smile.

He did not correct her and said, "And you are?"

"Fabiana."

"Is there anything I can do for you? Like, for example, I can show you the area if you want to. That's the least I can do."

"What do you mean?"

"Well, I always wanted to thank you for defending me. If you are free –"

Bored since moving to Jungle City, Fabiana took Johnny's bold move as a good sign. She said, "Okay. Meet me at my mother's catering business. The address is in the bill."

"Wait, did we pay this bill already?"

"No."

"Here you are." Johnny took cash from his wallet and asked the receptionist to write 'PAID' on the receipt. "Tomorrow, what time is good for you?"

"About four o'clock?" She asked.

He flashed a wide smile and nodded.

The next day, when Johnny ate Ceeda's mashed potatoes for lunch, he said, "Ceeda, no cook in the world matches your talent. You'll always be my favorite cook. However, I'm meeting an angel whose mother just started a catering business. Don't worry. There's room for many cooks in my life."

Ceeda beamed.

After a quick siesta nap, Johnny prepared to meet the Angel. As he walked toward the door, Ceeda said he was very handsome. He was about to turn the doorknob when the door opened up, and in came Glorieta. She sniffed the air. "What's with this stinking smell? Johnny, I asked you to get rid of your cheap cologne. Go. Take a shower."

"He has an important meeting," intervened Ceeda.

"With whom?"

"An angel," Johnny said.

"Her mother is a caterer," Ceeda volunteered.

"Don't tell me you are meeting Fabiana?"

"Yes, I am."

"In that case, you definitely have to shower my handsome son; to impress her. I have the right men's cologne I bought for Pr, huh, for you. Go! What are you waiting for? No time to waste discussing it." Glorieta pushed him towards the bathroom.

"Stop, Mom. It was just a fart. I'm going like this and will call a taxi to ..."

Hiding her irritation with a smile, Glorieta said, "Wait right here. I'll call Mike to see when your car is ready." Ignoring Johnny's protest that he had already called the mechanic, she went to her bedroom, dialed not the mechanic but a secret number, and whispered, "Great news!"... She listened. "Not yet. Be patient. Monlevade finally came back into town just a few days ago and gave me the drawings to the ranch. Yes, I trust him."... Glorieta stopped listening. Her mind was on her recent rendezvous with Monlevade. "My sugar," he said. Kissing her neck, he unbuttoned her silk shirt to bury his face on her plump chest. "I'm going to assess the area."

"Good. I'll keep this tube. But... wait a minute. Where's my guarantee?"

Monlevade drew attention to his handwritten equation on the top corner of the blueprint. Glorieta read aloud, savoring each word, "one-half minus mine equals one-half minus yours."

"Happy?" He asked.

"Ever the human calculator, aren't you? I'll write something better."

Glorieta returned her attention to the phone call. "If you keep interrupting, I won't tell you. Okay. Johnny is going out with Fabiana. For now, just pray that they date and marry. I'll fill you in with the details later."

After hanging up the phone, Glorieta picked up a gift box from the top drawer of her dresser. "I'll get you another one, Prestle." She said while unwrapping it and putting the Brut cologne in her purse. Returning to the living room, she held Johnny by the arm and said, "I'm taking you to Pearl's. You're going there, right? Come on. Let's go."

Resigned, Johnny looked at Ceeda, who was shaking her head. She said, "I know, no cab."

The thermometer on the Main street median indicated 100 degrees Fahrenheit. At the red light at a traffic light, while Johnny wiped off sweat from his face and busied himself in raising the air conditioning in the car, Glorieta quickly retrieved the Brut cologne, dropped the equivalent of a tablespoon on her hands, and tapped Johnny's neck, hair, and arms.

"Stop! I applied my own cologne." He tried to halt Glorieta's action to no avail.

"This one is top of the line. You'll smell like a prince. Stay indoors. Call me when you want to come back," she said and honked the horn for the car ahead of them to move.

"You don't need to come in, Mother. Please, don't come to pick me up, either."

"Okay, okay. Here we are. Go!" Glorieta dropped Johnny off and drove around the block. She parked on the opposite street, under a tree, out of Johnny's sight but with a good view of Pearl's business.

Sweaty Strolls and Sweet Moments

Fabiana was wearing a light long sleeve blouse and Khaki pants. She opened the front door and stepped outside because Lourdes was washing the floor with soap. "I don't want you to fall and break your neck," Fabiana teased. "Where to?"

Glorieta saw Johnny and Fabiana walk in the opposite direction from where she was parked. Her hands were on the steering wheel as she said aloud to herself, "Johnny, if you sweat like a pig, it's your fault. Haven't I told you to stay indoors?"

Johnny unbuttoned the top buttons of his shirt and fanned his face with his hands.

"*Brute,*" she said with a strong accent, taking a good whiff.

He smiled, slightly embarrassed, "Excuse me?"

"Your cologne. My dad, rest his soul, liked it."

"Ah! I see. I can only handle a ten-minute walk to the ice cream parlor in this hot weather if I'm wearing Brut. I don't want to mix cologne with sweat," he chuckled.

Johnny ordered the ice cream cones and Fabiana got them a table under a mango tree full of noisy green parakeets. Johnny offered her his ice cream, and she leaned in closer to taste it. They laughed at their clumsiness. "You have what I'd call a sweet chin," he said, pointing out the ice cream smudge on her chin.

Several drops of melted ice cream fell on Johnny's lap, staining his trousers. "Better this than bird's droppings," he said as he cleaned the mess with his napkin.

Johnny was sure he would walk Fabiana back to Pearl's catering business. He raised an eyebrow when Fabiana said it would be closed by now and that she lived about a thirty-minute walk from the ice cream parlor.

Johnny's forehead and chubby face were glistening with sweat. He brought his napkin to his face, and the napkin, with traces of ice cream, burned his eyes. "Water," he urged, squinting.

Fabiana walked to the cashier and asked for a glass of water. She came back and said, "Johnny, I'm sorry. I don't have one dollar."

"Hey, I don't care about drinking water. My eyes are burning. Tap water is fine. Tell the cashier I'll pay later. Hurry!"

Fabiana got a cup of water and napkins and suppressed laughing when Johnny tried to dip the napkin in the glass with closed eyes. "Here, let me do it," she said. He tilted his head back and let Fabiana apply the wet napkin on to his eyes. After a few minutes, he sighed in relief and said, "You are an angel. You saved me again."

When they reached Fabiana's home, their faces were red and visibly sweaty. They fanned themselves with their hands. To disguise his body odor, Johnny collected a rose from someone's garden and waved it under Fabiana's nose. "A rose for a rose. Smell it."

Fabiana brought Johnny to her art studio and showed him a few of her illustrations of geometric forms. Johnny raised his eyebrows, "Nice. But, to be honest, I don't understand any of these drawings."

The next few days, Johnny occasionally placed orders from Pearl's Catering for the bank. But he always got disappointed. Manuelito was the one delivering the food. Not the Angel. He called her. But his phone calls were never answered because Fabiana was out buying supplies for her art studio, dropping off food for her mother, or just sitting in her backyard watching the tropical birds in the sky.

When they finally connected by phone, Johnny said, "Fabiana. If you are not busy, would you like to go out for pizza? It can also be ice cream again."

"When?"

"I can pick you up in the next hour."

"I… okay."

"Who called?" Pearl entered the room and asked.

"A manager from the bank, Johnny."

"Johnny? He's Glorieta's son."

"Oh no! Seriously, son of that weird lady?" Manuelito teased.

"Come on, kids. Be nice. I have a lot to thank Glorieta for. What did Johnny want?"

"To go out for pizza."

"I'm cooking your favorite, darling. Squash *kibbeh.* Invite him to stay for dinner."

Johnny was delighted with the invitation and praised Pearl's culinary talent incessantly.

Over the next few months, Johnny alternated dinners prepared by Ceeda and Pearl. After dinner at Fabiana's house, he would sit down on the couch next to his Angel and watch the soap opera in silence under Pearl's watchful eyes.

One day, Fabiana spent almost an hour applying her make-up, and Johnny covered his eyes with his hands and said, "Oh, no. You and my mother can go out together." Another day, Fabiana ventured into preparing him coffee. He made a face and complained it was very sweet. He asked her to learn how to cook to help Pearl. She said her idea of helping her mother was simply to design some marketing materials.

Fabiana got annoyed with Johnny's comments and unflattering remarks. When she told him she had two things in mind - to work in tourism and travel the world, Johnny replied he didn't want her to work at all. That night, she lay down and recapped their conversation.

Johnny, I want to go to Rock in Rio. I'll get tickets.

Bee, how many times do I need to tell you I hate big cities?

I wanna go.

No, Bee, you don't.

I beg your pardon?

I said we are not going, Bee.

She switched the alarm's radio on, and some music played. "Okay, you goofball." She tossed in bed and a few minutes later blurted, "Outrageous!" The house was still. Fabiana needed some fresh air.

As her mother had warned her, if she ever needed to go to her studio in the backyard at night, she should take along some meat or grab the tranquilizer gun with her in case a wild animal was out there. She opened the kitchen door and checked her surroundings before heading for her studio.

She started drawing Johnny's eyes while mumbling to herself, "Our relationship is so bland. We don't kiss when we meet or when we say goodbye; we just sit in front of the TV for hours. We've never gone out dancing or to a live concert. You know what? I won't let anyone control me. I need to live my life."

***

After a few days, on Manuelito's twelfth birthday, he got gifts from Pearl and Fabiana. His sister drew a cartoon of him on his bike and signed it as a memorabilia. Pearl got him a birthday cake and surprised him with a Polaroid camera. It was used but in good condition. She had bartered it with one of her clients. That day, Manuelito took the first pictures with his new device, of his mom and Fabiana, and the three of them excitedly waited for the film to develop before their eyes. He was so happy and kept the Polaroid camera next to his old camera from Rio and the Pentax in his bedroom.

Jungle City, 1984

Rosettes

Padded paws moved on grassy grounds towards Fabiana's neighborhood.

The evening sky with dark cumulus clouds was intimidating. Heavy winds blew tree leaves and brought much-needed relief from the heat. The city lost electrical power.

As Fabiana lay in bed, a seesaw sound mingled with the loud thunder forced her out of bed. She picked up the flashlight that was always on her nightstand, headed toward the window, and peered outside scanning the area for a moment. The lightening hindered her visibility until she eventually identified a four-legged figure lurking behind a tree. *A Savannah cat?* She thought to herself before pointing the flashlight at it. As soon as the light reached the animal, it revealed its glassy-looking eyes and unique spots on its skin.

Fabiana skipped a heartbeat. She knew what she had seen but did not want to accept it. It seemed as if she was unable to move her legs as the beast stared back at her. A few seconds later, the animal ran away behind a capybara.

"Rosettes! It's a jaguar. Dear Lord, help us!" It took a few seconds for Fabiana to calm her racing heart after the jaguar had left.

The next morning, carrying a morsel of meat, Fabiana entered the studio and drew rosettes and cat's eyes. Pearl came over to say Clara was on the phone. Before stepping outside, Fabiana looked around. She told her mom about the jaguar. Alarmed, Pearl embraced her daughter. Looking around for any sign of danger, they stepped inside the kitchen and Fabiana answered her childhood girlfriend. She nodded several times and said she would watch for the mail.

Everyday, Fabiana checked the mailbox for Clara's mail. While anticipating the letter, Fabiana, in a spontaneous moment, repeatedly packed her suitcase on the bed. Manuelito passed by her bedroom, curious about her actions. Inviting him in, she implored him to care for their mother and remain vigilant. After a heartfelt hug, Fabiana revealed her decision to leave Jungle City.

Manuelito, puzzled, questioned her dislike for jungle life. She confided that she felt she was losing her sanity, and recounted the jaguar sighting. Manuelito reassured her about jaguars and said, "I've read that jaguars typically only attack humans if they feel threatened or provoked. They're known to be elusive and prefer avoiding confrontations. Maybe the encounter was rare."

Fabiana disclosed her need for money and her plan to use education funds. Manuelito suggested selling her ranch, but she explained her promise to her grandfather. When Manuelito asked her about marrying Johnny, Fabiana urged her brother not to be narrow-minded like some in the jungle. Determined, she announced her intention to eventually conquer the world.

When the letter arrived, Fabiana propped herself on her bed to read it. Clara had mailed the page of a magazine called *Manchete* and attached a note saying, "I'm enrolled. Would you be interested?"

Fabiana read the information with interest. A tourism school had opened registration for their five-month session starting in September and guaranteed job positions to the students by placing them in prestigious tour companies and airlines. Candidates needed to know English and if placed as stewardesses, they also had to be tall and not wear eyeglasses. Fabiana knew her English was not perfect but she was tall. She straightened herself up and rushed to take her shower.

Standing before a mirror on her closet door afterward, she went a bit overboard applying a vibrant green eyeshadow. Satisfied with the makeup, she combed her short brown hair in various directions before taming it with a barrette. Wearing a blue suit, skirt, matching pumps, and exuding confidence, she went to the dining room, pulled up a chair, and waited for Manuelito. When he got home from delivering food to his mother's clients, he was drenched in sweat. Fabiana delicately put her fingers on his shoulder, brought him to her bedroom, closed the door, and stood against it.

"My dear brother," she said, "don't make a scene…. I have your Polaroid camera."

"Why?"

"I need a favor. If you help me, I'll help you go to the Rock in Rio."

"Okay. In that case, what do you need?"

"Take a picture of me against this door."

"Why?"

"Just do it."

"One only," he said, taking the picture and handing her the black film that was sliding out of the Polaroid camera. He was about to open the door to leave the room but Fabiana closed it again. Examining the Polaroid picture that was coming into view, she said, "Please, take another one, will you? This picture doesn't show the whole door."

"No. Mom won't buy me more Polaroid films. It's expensive."

"But look at this picture. You cut the door, see? What I want is me against the whole door, get it?" She tossed the picture on the bed.

"Why are you fussing about the door?" He looked at the picture on the bed. "You look nice in this picture."

"I just want to show my height. I want them to see that I'm as tall as a standard door."

"Them, who? Who's going to see the pictures?"

"I'll tell you if you promise not to tell Mom, Johnny, or anybody."

Manuelito did not seem to care, shrugged his shoulders, and said, "Okay."

"The Institute people." Fabiana confided excitedly. "I'm going to study and have them place me at Pan Am. I need to send them a picture showing that I'm a tall person."

"You gotta tell Mom."

"I'll tell her if I get the job. So, the picture has to be good. Come on. Take another, will ya?"

They heard Pearl's voice as she entered the living room, "Kids, I'm home."

"Manuelito, you promised. Not a word to her about this."

Pearl was feeling exhausted because of the heatwave. Turning on the fan in the living room, she sat down on the sofa and waved her cotton shirt to cool off herself.

"Hi, darlings," she said when the siblings entered the living room.

"Hi, Mom." They did not sound enthusiastic.

"Everything okay? What are you two doing? Fabiana, what's it with the green eyeshadow?"

"Nothing. Manuelito needs to do his homework, and I'm going to help him."

"You two are so good together. I pray you'll always be together to help one another."

"But, Mom," Manuelito complained with a dramatic tone in his voice, "if Fabiana moves away, I don't wanna go with her."

Fabiana's brown eyes darted in his direction.

"Nobody's moving, dear. Ah! Fabiana, I have good news for you. Before leaving work today, I had a nice conversation about you with one of my clients."

"About me? Why?"

"Well, I told this client you're looking to earn extra money and guess what?"

"What? I am not looking for any job here. I already help you, Mom."

"I know. Anyway, the veterinarian told me she'd be happy to have you onboard assisting her. You'd be the 'veterinarian assistant'! Isn't it great? And I know exactly what you can do there."

"Mom, you know I don't want to work with animals."

"No darling, you're good with organizing, so I think she wants you to go over the daily inventory of, oh, I don't know, something, and-"

"I think the veterinarian needs someone who is cut out to do the job. Please tell her thank you, but no thank you."

"She's going to be a Pan Am stewardess, Mom." Manuelito teased.

"Stop it, you goofball," Fabiana reprimanded him.

"Pan Am? But there's no Pan Am office here. Isn't it in Sao Paulo? Rio? New York?"

"Yeah. Actually, I want to apply to study tourism in Rio. Wait a minute." She went to her bedroom, picked up the *Manchete* article, and showed it to Pearl. "See, this Institute can place me at Pan Am offices – here first, then move on to New York City. It's my dream, Mom."

"I took a picture of her against the door so she can show Pan Am people that she's tall."

"Remember, son, Polaroid film is expensive," said Pearl.

"I told her so."

"Darling, why go back to Rio? I don't think it's a good thing to do."

"I," she hesitated. "Forget about Rock in Rio," she first snapped at her brother. "Mom, I am applying to the school because I want to travel the entire globe and immerse myself in diverse cultures. Pan Am stewardesses speak English and are tall and gorgeous, just like me."

"You're tall and speak English, alright. Gorgeous? Ha, ha."

"Manuelito, enough teasing. Let's think about it, okay?"

"Mom, I contacted Clara. She is already enrolled and said I can initially live with her and her husband."

"Really? It won't be good to live with newlyweds. You should stay here."

"I've been waiting for a course like this all my life, Mom. I can finally put the money in my trust to good use."

After fanning herself, Pearl said, "How about Rancho Santa Fabiana? How about Johnny?"

"We are not serious. He's in Campo Grande attending training during this entire month. He didn't even tell me about it himself. I learned from his secretary. I made up my mind, Mom. I don't want the ranch. If Grandpa wanted me to take care of it, he made a mistake. It requires maintenance money, which we don't have. And Johnny, well, he will have to understand. I'm going to enroll and book my reservations."

The next week, Fabiana showed her tickets to Pearl and nodded as her mother read, "Jungle City to Campo Grande, September first, at midnight, and VARIG flight from Campo Grande to Rio de Janeiro, round trip, next day at six in the evening. Returning in January. I see. In that case, okay, darling."

***

It was in Campo Grande that Johnny bought an engagement ring. "I'll propose when I return to Jungle City," he said to the salesperson. He had spent a month away from Jungle City, his favorite place in the world.

It was raining cats and dogs. When Johnny got home, he stood outside the cab waiting for his change. Ceeda was looking through the window and opened the door to him.

Before going to his bedroom, he opened the blue box and showed the ring to Ceeda, who beamed. She congratulated him, scolded him for being caught in the torrential rain without an umbrella, and wished him a good night's sleep.

Johnny paced his bedroom. Unexpectedly, he fell ill, experiencing both a bloody nose and abdominal pain. Without

45

changing out of his damp street clothes, he lay down and slept, holding the blue ring box close to his heart. While a bloody nose isn't usually a clear sign of leukemia, Johnny was familiar with the symptoms of bruising and bleeding. He had dealt with nosebleeds since childhood and had been diagnosed with early-stage leukemia at the age of sixteen, receiving treatment.

Two days later, feeling somewhat improved, Johnny decided to visit Fabiana and propose. To his disappointment, Manuelito conveyed that he had missed her by a couple of days. Standing at Fabiana's front door, Johnny looked disheartened.

1984 - Journey to Dreams
From Jungle to City Skies

The rain that fell that night brought little relief from the heat. Fabiana hugged and waved goodbye to her mother and brother, entered a cab, and proceeded to the bus station. After taking her window seat, she slept right away during the overnight trip to Campo Grande. In the morning, she called Madame Sophia but got her answering machine stating that she was out of town. She went straight to the airport, sat down in the waiting area, took a nap on the chair, and was the first in line when her VARIG flight was called.

The VARIG Airlines crew greeted the passengers boarding the three-hour flight from Campo Grande to Rio de Janeiro. Fabiana looked at her boarding ticket, stopped at her assigned seat, and tried to accommodate her cosmetic case in the overhead bin. It didn't seem to fit in. A stewardess approached and helped her place it in the next overhead bin. While thanking the stewardess, Fabiana discreetly admired the stewardess's makeup and her light blue uniform. She wanted to pick up every detail. After all, she was on her way to study tourism at the tour institute in the big city.

She did not mind the middle seat. A grandmotherly figure was already at the window. Nodding, Fabiana said, "Leaving Jungle City and going back to Rio for good, this time." The woman stopped reading the safety information card and watched Fabiana fasten her seat belt. Fabiana continued, "I can hardly wait for the wonderful things I'll do after reaching the fast-paced city of Rio."

Glancing at her over her eyeglasses, the woman gave a tentative smile and returned to her reading. When it became clear the aisle seat was empty, Fabiana moved over to it and smiled to herself. She was on her way. She was going to get hired in the tourism field and get paid to travel the world. But also high on her agenda was meeting interesting people. A new boyfriend? That would be a bonus.

Thinking about Johnny, the ex-boyfriend she had left behind, she realized, "Clearly a jungle guy at heart. We would never live in the big city. With him, that is out of the question. No. No regrets."

During the inflight meal, Fabiana admired the tray with a cup and cutlery displaying the VARIG Airlines logo. She refrained from putting them in her bag and remained quiet when the stewardess came to collect the items.

***

After retrieving her luggage in the carousel at Santos Dumont Airport, Fabiana proceeded to the exit gate and, with a big smile, opened her arms to embrace her childhood girlfriend, Clara.

"I can't believe we are going to school together again. So happy you are back. Stay as long as you need," Clara said while placing Fabiana's luggage in the trunk of her husband's small, two-door station wagon.

"Until the end of the course? Five months is not too long?"

Clara started driving and shook her head.

Unsure whether Clara had shaken her head in response to her first or second question, Fabiana stared and said, "Are you sure? I'll be happy to share expenses."

Looking both ways and paying attention to the chaotic traffic, Clara said, "Damn bad drivers! Did you see that? That guy just cut in front of me. Will you rent a car?" Fabiana shook her head. Clara continued, "Okay. So, let's do this. My husband will drive both of us to the institute in the morning. When he can't do that, we'll ride the bus. Just pay for gas and get the groceries. How about that?"

Fabiana opened the window and said to the skies, "Sure. Yeah! Rio, I'm back. I should never have left you. Rio, I love you." At Fabiana's request, they stopped at a shopping center. She bought flowers and gifts for the couple, then shopped for a hairdryer and a recording device for the classes. Citing purse-snatching incidents, Clara advised Fabiana against buying the Walkman.

"I assure you, Clara, that I'll be careful and use it mainly at the institute," Fabiana said, buying the Walkman. After paying, she concealed it in the pocket of her white Dijon metallic jeans, the latest trend in fashion.

Standing at the entrance door of Clara's studio, Fabiana tried to dismiss a rising thought. *So nice of Clara to offer it, but a newlywed's one-bedroom house is not the best place for long-term visitors,* Fabiana's mother had said while pouring both of them a cup of freshly brewed coffee just a few days ago in their home in Jungle City. Fabiana said she did not mind the open area that doubled as a living room and kitchenette. Receiving instructions to stack her belongings in the space between the couch, which would be her bed, and the TV shelf, she said, "Lovely! Thank you for having me, Clara."

From the start, Clara's husband had been annoyed. In private, to convince him to let Fabiana stay with them, Clara had promised him they would have gourmet groceries in return. He became less and less talkative as the weeks went by, despite Fabiana and Clara's efforts to select the expensive groceries her husband liked to eat.

One day, while resting on the couch, Fabiana could not help but overhear the couple arguing in their bedroom. Clara's voice was muffled but her husband's audible enough. "You know damn well that I don't let my own family spend even a weekend with us."

"Lower your voice. She is my childhood friend."

"I don't care. How long is the jungle girl going to stay?"

Fabiana lightly bit her lips. That same day, she went out, bought a newspaper, and perused the classified section. She visited a few of the bedrooms listed for rent and moved out two days later.

The relieved expression in the husband's eyes and Clara's apologetic gaze did not escape Fabiana's attention.

***

The bedroom in the farm-like house located an hour away from the institute would serve her well for now. In the meantime, she would continue to look for a better place.

After receiving the rental payment for October and November, the unshaved landlord asked Fabiana to choose one of the two beds and one of the two closets in the room. He told her he expected to rent the second bed and closet anytime soon. Winking an eye, he said, "Let's hope for a nice woman like yourself." Biting her lips, Fabiana put the contents of her luggage and makeup case in her assigned closet and went to bed, holding tears and hugging her pillow.

A stack of paintings and photographs in a corner of the room caught her attention. She looked through them and lifted one of the photos. A jaguar resting with its cubs in a dense jungle was looking at her. The intensity of the jaguar's eyes made Fabiana think of her recent encounter with a jaguar and of her grandfather who had lived and died in Jungle City. He had taught her and Manuelito a few survival techniques if they ever encountered wild animals in the jungle.

Fabiana used the long bus commuting time to study and listen to her Walkman that she kept concealed in the pocket of her jeans. One day, nearing her stop, she removed the Walkman earphones and put them in her purse. She noticed too late that her Walkman was no longer in her pocket. She was ashamed to tell Clara that the Walkman was gone and appreciated the fact that Clara didn't say, "I said so."

A Rainy Encounter

In late November, at the end of their Event Leadership class, Fabiana said goodbye to Clara and lingered in the institute to peruse guide books in the room adjacent to counselor Janice's office. For a few seconds, her curious eyes met the gaze of an athletic young man who was speaking with Janice in English. "This is great! We'll be in touch," the foreigner said, coming towards Fabiana. She turned her attention to the bookshelves but looked furtively at him as he passed by.

A few minutes later, Fabiana left the building in time to see her bus approaching on the opposite side of the street. It was raining and she had no umbrella. A taxi seemed to stop for her, but before she got to it, someone else opened it, causing her to topple backward in slow motion. She hit the back of her head on a man's torso, who helped her to stand up. He held his briefcase over their head to protect both of them from the rain, but it only served to make them slightly wetter. Fabiana's clothes were now sticking to her body and she started to worry that people were seeing her clinging T-shirt. To protect herself, she crossed her backpack over her torso.

The man and Fabiana rushed back to the institute building hall. He opened his briefcase, retrieved a small round package, and offered it to her.

Fabiana could hear her mother's words: *Never accept things from strangers.* Shaking the water from her hair, she raised her eyebrows as if to ask, "What is this?"

Counselor Janice surprised the two of them by walking up and pointing to the package in Fabiana's hands, "Hello again! Awful summer rain, isn't it? Ah! Fabiana, you'll absolutely love it. Thanks again, Paolo. By the way, young man, two things. One, please make sure to use the restaurant voucher I gave you and recommend it to your clients. Two, this is the girl I spoke to you about. Gotta go. I see my husband's car right over there. He can't stand going around the block trying to find parking. Bye, *tchau*."

Fabiana shook her head, faked a smile, and played with her wet hair. Directing her attention to the package, she asked, "So, what is it?"

"Something I think you need. Open and see it for yourself."

Fabiana took the small package, shook it, and then simply held it while looking outside through the glass doors to see if another bus was approaching. She noticed the young foreigner motioning for her to open the round package, and she did. The small item turned into a bath towel depicting the Christ the Redeemer statue atop the mountain overlooking Copacabana bay and the slogan of his company. Admiring the towel, she said, "I love this image. What a great promotional product," she dried and covered herself, saying that she appreciated it.

He smiled and said, "I need one myself."

"Nice! Let me see yours… the Copacabana sidewalk. Very nice," she remarked when he dried his face and his hair and rested the towel on his shoulders. She couldn't pinpoint it, but there was something about his wet hair and his piercing gaze that made her heart skip.

"I'm Paolo."

"Italian?"

"American. And you?"

"Fabiana," she said.

"You were at the Institute," he pointed a thumb up and toward the counselor's floor.

"I'm graduating in January. How about you?"

"I'm a rep. I visit schools on behalf of Rio by Night Tours and bring these promotional products."

"Fantastic!"

"No tour tonight… It looks like this rain will last for hours. And like the counselor said, you are the one I need to speak to. Would you care for something to drink?"

Again, her mother's warning, *Keep an eye on your drink at all times,* flashed in her mind. "Where? These bars around here must be packed – everyone's trying to get out of the rain." Paolo looked at the restaurant voucher in his hand. "What would you say if we ran in the rain to make a dash for the Italian restaurant at the corner?"

Wondering if she was doing the right thing, she said, "That's fine." She couldn't believe she had just accepted a stranger's invitation.

"Ready? I've got more towels just in case," he chuckled.

They ran, laughing. The water dripped from the wet towels on their heads and shoulders. In front of the restaurant, they wrung out the water from the wet towels. Once inside, Paolo pulled out two new promotional packages and they proceeded to dry themselves. They followed the waiter to a table by the window covered with a red and white plaid tablecloth, where they watched a colorful parade of umbrellas and cars splashing water on the pavement. Gradually, the darkness of the evening was replaced by bright neon signs outside. They read the menu and ordered wine and pizza. As their glasses clinked together, they toasted, "Cheers to good food, good company, good music." Their focus then shifted to the approaching guitar player serenading them with "Oh! Sole Mio."

One glass of wine might have been enough for Fabiana, but she allowed the waiter to pour a second glass for her. "A toast to laughter," she proposed. Fabiana didn't want the fun to end, but when the waiter approached for the third refill, she decided it was time to leave. Paolo asked her where she lived, and upon her response, he hailed a cab for her. As she entered the cab, he gave her his business card. Unaware of her new home's number, Fabiana assured him she would be in touch. As the taxi drove away, she realized she did not know what he wanted to talk about with her.

***

Two days later, Sunday was a perfect day to go out. Fabiana thought of Paolo. Stepping into the nearest public telephone booth on the sidewalk, looking at the business card, she debated on whether to call him or not. She didn't want to give him the wrong impression of her, but she was yearning for some company.

Paolo was standing in his favorite spot, looking out the window of his beach apartment. He could see the Christ the Redeemer statue in the distance. The telephone on the night table rang. He gulped his beer and sat down on the bed. Yes, he was available to go out. He was happy to hear from Fabiana and suggested they meet at the shopping center convenient for both of them.

Back in her room, Fabiana tried on several outfits before settling on an animal print blouse and shorts combo with matching shoes. She finished off the look with her favorite fragrance - the Charlie perfume, which was advertised in its alluring TV ad as representing the bold and brave new woman of the 1980s.

At the meeting point, looking at her reflection on the mirrored wall, Fabiana fluffed her hair for the nth time. When she saw Paolo coming towards her, she thought he was so good-looking in his choice of clothing. He was wearing a Polo shirt, shorts and tennis shoes. They ate burgers and beers and laughed a lot. Passing by the bowling alley on the street level of the shopping center, Paolo convinced Fabiana to play. He was an excellent bowler. Fabiana was playing it for the first time. He helped her hold the bowling ball, and she liked the feel of his warm hands on hers. They high-fived when Fabiana hit one of the pins. It was their second date and both of them were enjoying themselves.

As soon as they were done with bowling, Paolo and Fabiana decided to go to a Disco Club located on the shopping center's top floor. As they neared the club, their faces were illuminated by neon lights and a disco ball, and they could hear the speakers playing some iconic tunes from the 1980s. As they tried walking past the bouncer, they were stopped.

"You can't enter in shorts," the bouncer said in his low-pitched voice. Determined, they went into a store selling disco clothing on the floor below and bought bellbottom trousers for Paolo and a psychedelic midi skirt with a side slit for Fabiana. Paolo paid for the purchase despite Fabiana's objection but Paolo insisted. With their disco attire, they returned to the club and, during Donna Summer's "Let's Dance," they shared a kiss that left Fabiana fascinated.

Fabiana didn't want the fun to stop. They sat down, ordered drinks, and tried hard to hear each other above the noise. The booming music at the club forced her to speak louder when she asked, "Have you ever been to Jungle City?"

Paolo took a moment to answer. "I may have to go over there. Do you by any chance know anybody called John P. Iva.?" She shook her head, not because she had an answer, but because she couldn't catch the question. Paolo remained quiet and finished his beer. It was getting late and he was debating whether to take her home or not. Fabiana lived in an undesirable neighborhood, and as a foreigner, he had heard horror stories about the area. Leaving the club, he hailed a cab for her, and they shared a kiss. She then stepped into the cab, her eyes sparkling with stars.

Paolo had just opened the door to his apartment when the phone started ringing. He answered and said, "Really? A tour job in the Pantanal? Yes. I'm interested. Starting when? Sure, I can start as early as this week. Thank you, Greg." After ending the call, he dialed the airline company and booked his flight to the Pantanal, where he would be starting his new tour job.

Fabiana felt sure they had struck a connection. She longed for Paolo and wrote a handwritten love letter to him - which she kept in her cosmetic case. Fabiana's love letter included their shared moments on their dates and perhaps a promise of lasting love in the style of classic romantic films. The letter was adorned with the eyes of Paolo and eyes of the jaguar, sprayed with a hint of her favorite Charlie perfume and sealed with a heartfelt phrase: *In the symphony of life, your love is my favorite melody."* But to her dismay, her next phone calls to Paolo went unanswered. And soon, it was Christmas.

***

In the early morning, the cup of coffee failed to produce the desired effect for Paolo. Hoping to stay alert for a morning beach visit, he returned to bed instead, aiming to save his energy for the upcoming travel later in the day.

The phone rang and Paolo woke up. The digital radio clock now indicated 10:45 AM. He answered with a sleepy voice. The operator said, "This is an international call from Boston for Mr. Paolo Sendal."

"This is him."

"Please, hold. Mrs. Sendal, Mr. Sendal is on the line."

"Paolo, it's Gram. Did I wake you up? How are you doing, dear?"

"No, Gram. Doing good. I was thinking of you. Sorry, I could not be there to celebrate Grampa's first year since his passing. How did it go?"

Margrit said, "Paolo, I still can't believe he's gone. He lives in our memories."

Immersed in images of Papps, his late grandfather, Paolo yearned to be there for his grandma, offering the same comforting embrace that Papps used to provide. In a poignant recollection, young Paolo returned home from elementary school to discover that a wild coyote had taken the life of his beloved pet. Still vivid in his mind was the moment Papps hugged him, reassuring "Your dog is in Dog Heaven."

"Gram, I'm so sorry."

She said, "Paolo, please don't be mad."

"Why would I be?" Paolo asked gently.

"I found Caroline's diary."

"Gram! Why did you go over my boxes in the attic?"

"I had to. I was looking for pictures of Papps with you. I was also mad at myself for misplacing Caroline's diary. And what a relief when I found it among your things…"

"Gram, I wanted to find out about my father's whereabouts, and I would tell you only after finding him."

"We met him, John, having lunch with Caroline at Quincy Market. Said he was on his school break. They broke up before Caroline knew she was pregnant with you."

"I know."

"When you were born, we promised Caroline that we would care for you. In her diary, she wrote that your father had got an internship over there. Her letters to him had returned undeliverable. So, according to Caroline, he disappeared without a trace."

The thought of a few envelopes addressed to John P. Iva, Brazil's Forest Service, Rio de Janeiro, popped into his mind. Paolo left them where he found them, in a file box in the attic. Margrit had labeled 'Our Darling'.

"That's why I'm here. I've been searching for him without success. My sources were wrong. They said there was a John P. Iva in Rio, but he might be in the Pantanal."

"Oh!" Margrit seemed surprised.

Paolo combed his tousled hair with his finger, and mentioned his upcoming trip to the Pantanal.

Margit wished him good luck.

After hanging up the phone, Paolo said a silent prayer to Papps, the man who taught him boy scouts survival skills.

 Caroline, their only daughter, his mother, died peacefully and unexpectedly of a brain aneurysm six months after giving birth to Paolo. His grandparents tried to make his father's absence as painless as possible and kept their daughter's diary away from Paolo's eyes. Until the day he found it in a box labeled 'Our Darling,' read it, and kept it in a box marked 'Paolo school stuff.'

Paolo remembered the day he sat in the attic reading it. Caroline had written that the baby's father, John P. Iva, had been her first and only boyfriend.

It was by sheer coincidence that Margrit found it in Paolo's box in the attic. She was apologetic, but she should not have been. Paolo was glad that now his grandmother knew why he had come to Brazil.

Recalling the hours spent in Gram's attic, reading his mom's diary brought back mixed emotions about the man who abandoned him and his dying mother. She had clearly written his name and that he had been her only boyfriend. The only thing she didn't have was his correct overseas address. All she wrote was that John's flight would bring him to the Forest Services and, per some digging, decided its office was in Rio.

Upon learning the name of his father, Paolo decided to come to Rio. While searching for him, he envisioned living by the beach and learning a little Portuguese. Soon, he came across the ad about this hard-to-believe penthouse rental deal. The only drawback was that the penthouse was sandwiched between two taller buildings and didn't face the beach. However, he could enjoy a peek at the Christ the Redeemer statue atop Corcovado Mountain from his bedroom window. Initially, he regretted signing the rental agreement for six months. Now that he was going to the Pantanal, he was relieved that the rent was ending at the end of the month.

He thought about his job. It was also a relief that it was not a permanent position. Through his college alma mater connections and mainly because of his English skills and knowledge of Brazilian History, right upon his arrival, he got a freelance job as a private tour guide catering to hotel guests.

A growling sound in the pit of his stomach reminded him that he had not eaten anything yet. He opened the refrigerator and stared at semi-empty shelves, if not for a few bottles of Brahma beer, a Brazilian brand that he liked very much, and soft tomatoes. He saw a stale piece of bread on the counter by a ceramic teapot.

Massaging his chin, Paolo stopped at the window overlooking his favorite bakery, where he always stopped for breakfast.

He called the airlines regarding his reservation for Rio-Campo Grande and the line was busy. While waiting to call again, he recalled his earlier conversation with this source.

"Paolo, I've got news for you." said the male voice. "There's a Mr. P. Iva in the Pantanal."

"Do you have his address?"

"That's the problem. All I could uncover from a hospital an hour from Jungle City is that a certain Mr. P. Iva was treated for fire inhalation several years ago. 1972, to be precise. I want to know if you want me to follow this lead."

"No. Thank you for everything. I'll take care from here." He listened and replied, "That's fine. I'll deposit the money into your account."

Paolo took a shower and reconfirmed his intentions. He won't change his trip nor extend the apartment leasing. The problem at hand now was Fabiana. Deep down, he regretted not having a phone number or address to contact her over the holidays.

He turned off the shower faucet and watched the water go down the drain of the bathroom floor.

The Jaguar's Gamble And Unravelling Charades

Much to Fabiana's disappointment, Paolo didn't respond to her phone calls after their second date. Before she knew it, Christmas had arrived.

Clara invited her to spend Christmas Eve with her and her husband. Fabiana accepted the invitation and, careful not to annoy Clara's husband, enjoyed the quiet dinner. Clara's husband had just installed a landline telephone and was complaining about how expensive it had been to obtain the telephone number. Fabiana asked Clara's permission to use the phone to call her mother and brother and, seeing Clara's husband slightly raise an eyebrow, offered to pay for the long-distance expense.

After assuring her mom that all was good and that she missed her and Manuelito, Fabiana passed the phone to Clara, who was motioning to let her speak with Pearl. "Hi, Pearl!... I miss you, too….Yes, me too. I have so many fond memories from the time you guys lived here. Very happy Fabiana is back… Don't worry about her; she will be just fine."

Pearl thanked Clara for letting Fabiana stay with her and was surprised to learn that Fabiana was not living with them. Equally surprised, Clara returned the phone to Fabiana and mouthed, "Your mom didn't know you moved?" Fabiana eased her mom's worries by saying that everything was fine and under control.

Fabiana stepped into a cab and headed home, feeling sadness. She silently prayed that New Year's Eve would bring her closer to Paolo. In her mind, she envisioned his hazel eyes morphing with the jaguar's amber eyes. She whispered, *Where are you, Paolo*?

***

In Jungle City, at the end of December, Monlevade sped down the unpaved road and raised heavy dust behind. He was fast approaching the long stretch of a swamp to his right, full of jabirus, the symbolic bird of the Brazilian wetlands. These flamingo-like birds with white plumage, black head, and a pink band on the base of their neck were peacefully feasting on whatever they could find in the still, green waters.

"Dinner time, huh? Hey birds, grab a big fish for me." Monlevade shouted as loud as he could, as if the birds could hear him.

He braked and skidded to a crawl. Pushing his straw hat up, Monlevade squinted, blinked, and stared. The pink-colored band on the bird's neck was turning a deep red scarlet color. When the birds' neck bands change color, they are agitated. He saw the birds take flight off, altogether *en masse*. Instead of marveling at their perfectly choreographed flight pattern, he ducked. The birds flew above and ahead of his truck, returning to their nests high in the trees at the end of the road.

He wondered what startled the birds. As they perched on the branches of tall trees and above him, he hit the dashboard as if suddenly understanding the birds' behavior.

"I'll be darned!" Monlevade yelled, "Hey, birds! You recognize my tree-trimming truck, huh? He tapped the steering wheel. "Birds, my company, Sandy Lagoons and I need *dinero*! To invest more. You can find houses in other trees. Plenty of trees around here."

Monlevade, a short-groomed man of humble origins who invested in abandoned properties via his company, Sandy Lagoons, retrieved his wallet from the pocket of his wrinkled shirt. He placed the wallet on his lap and managed to take a piece of paper from it while he pressed on the gas. He read RANCHO SANTA FABIANA. Looking around the plush vegetation, he addressed the birds perching on the trees at the farm toward the end of the road. "Yeah, birds! I think you are occupying the trees that I will cut. Sleep tight tonight and find other trees during the day tomorrow 'cause when you come back, those trees will be gone."

He looked at the sky. Gray cumulus clouds suddenly replaced the sunset hues of orange and red. Heavy drops of rain started to hit the truck's window. The heavy summer rain soon overpowered the windshield wipers, obfuscating Monlevade's vision.

He didn't bother with the decaying signs indicating PRIV---- P--PERTY - -- TRESPASSIN-. He leaned forward and peered through the wipers to read the metal sign hanging above the gateless entrance half a kilometer away. He stepped on the gas and said, "Rancho Santa Fabiana, site of my future resort… What the heck!"

Out of nowhere, a capybara crossed the road in front of the truck. Like a deer frozen by headlights, the capybara stared at the driver. To avoid full impact, Monlevade swerved to the right and, unable to slow down, ended up in the swamp.

Inoperable, the truck floated and rocked gently from side to side. Afraid that his truck might submerge, Monlevade opened the door to escape. His wallet fell from his lap onto the water. He was about to leave the vehicle when a vision in his rear mirror made him change his mind. Trembling, he quickly fumbled with the buttons and levers of the door to lock himself in the stuck truck. In his sixty years of living in the jungle, this was the first time he saw a jaguar come out of the lush vegetation.

"I'll be darned." He made the sign of the cross many times over his head and torso.

The rain stopped and a large rainbow appeared on the horizon. But again, the driver couldn't enjoy the view with the beast closing in. He watched the jaguar leap toward his truck. Feeling an intense pain, Monlevade brought his hands to his heart. *"My Lord"* was his last thought. He could no longer see the jaguar carrying the dead capybara and disappearing into the jungle.

***

Unaware of Monlevade's tragic demise a week ago, Glorieta lingered in bed, her eyes blackened with dried mascara, "It's just a matter of time now."

Inspecting her outfits in front of a long mirror, she said, "Time to impress. Mrs. Camargo, here I come," and danced to an imaginary *cha-cha-cha* tune. After discarding many expensive outfits on the bed, Glorieta decided on the brand-new plaid suit with huge shoulder pads. She accessorized the jacket with a colossal satin flower on the lapel. She was on her way to pick up the bank's newest and wealthiest client for lunch at an elegant restaurant.

She'd been given the assignment by Prestle, the septuagenarian V.P. of the only bank in Jungle City. He also happened to be Gloria's secret lover. Prestle had given Glorieta a large sum of cash to pay for the lunch. He had booked the restaurant and had informed Mrs. Camargo that Glorieta, the bank Welcome Relations Authority, would be picking her up before noon on this day.

Glorieta loved these types of assignments and always obliged. Prestle gave her an additional stipend with a single request. She was to go shopping and surprise him with her purchase of lacy underwear. "You pervert! I'm delighted," she squeezed the tip of his nose and left his office, undulating her body to the imaginary sound of her own cha-cha-cha.

After applying a heavy coat of makeup and mascara, Glorieta sprayed a very expensive perfume on her hair, neck, and wrists and left the house to meet Mrs. Camargo. She parked her Mercedes and covered her wide open mouth with her hand when she realized the Camargo's mansion occupied half of the street block. The maid let her in. While waiting, Glorieta took in the impressive redwood paneling of the entrance hall, the ugly abstract paintings on the walls, and the expensive furniture in the living room. She noticed a great number of fresh flower arrangements scattered around the room. *I shall have a home like this one day. Monlevade promised me.*

"Wow!" Glorieta complimented the bank's elegant client, who entered the room with a confident smile. "You look amazing. What a nice hair color. I shall go to your hairdresser."

Mrs. Camargo, adorned with lots of fashion jewelry, fluffed her hair and said, "My hairdresser is closed today. Her boyfriend died in the swamp by Rancho Santa Fabiana a week ago."

"Who was he?"

"Monlevade. Not to speak ill of the dead, but he was a reclusive, filthy, unscrupulous man who cheated in the past." Did you know him? He had a heart attack."

Glorieta swayed and reached out to steady herself on one of the flower pedestals, almost knocking it over. She whispered, "Oh!" She said while recalling the words Monlevade had whispered in her ears the last time they met. *Your financial woes will soon be over. I'll take care of you.*

"The funeral was two days ago. My hairdresser, Monlevade's girlfriend, received so many flowers that she gave me a few. They are beautiful, aren't they?"

"Your hair is beautiful."

"Thank you." Mrs. Camargo patted her curls. "I don't know how people can afford her. She uses the trendiest products. Says she orders products straight from the capital."

Son of a Grinch! She's implying I can't afford her hairdresser.

Shaken by the information that Monlevade was dead and that he had more than one girlfriend, combined with this rich bitch's not-so-subtle insult, Glorieta had a sudden change of heart. "Look, I came to say I can't go out for lunch."

"Why didn't you call?"

"I wasn't home. I'm not one to use the public *Orelhão*, referring to the ear-shaped phone booths found on the sidewalks all over Brazil. I just came to say hello, welcome you to the bank, and goodbye."

"How about a cup of coffee?"

"No, I gotta go."

Double-Crossed Affairs And Whispers of Betrayal

Monlevade is dead. This thought hit the pit of Glorieta's stomach. In her haste to leave, she almost tripped on the Italian mosaic staircase leading to the street. Waving goodbye, Glorieta sought comfort inside her car. She drove away, and as soon as she turned out of sight, she parked again.

It wasn't so much that Monlevade had another secret lover. She was fuming because he had left some unfinished business behind. She'd planned on taking possession of half of Rancho Santa Fabiana. She hit the steering wheel. "Monlevade, were you going to share what is mine with someone else? You bastard, we had a plan. Now, you're dead. What am I going to do?"

Glorieta gave a huge sigh, composed herself, and assessed her image in the rearview mirror of her car. After tidying up her messy makeup and applying another coat of mascara, she started the car and drove to the bank. Prestle was surprised to see her back so soon.

"There was no lunch," Glorieta snapped. "Did you know Monlevade passed away?"

"No. Just a week ago, he was seated in that chair, trying to catch his breath. I urged him to see a doctor. I even offered to have my secretary check his blood pressure. He changed the subject and told me he was going to invest in an abandoned ranch."

"It's not abandoned, Prestle. It belongs to Fabia--. Hey, come to think about it, the ranch is abandoned." Glorieta paced the office. "I need a drink." Prestle offered whisky on the rocks. She gulped it.

"Fabiana's grouchy grandfather made me believe he had no family and that he was leaving the ranch to me. One day, his estranged daughter and her two kids appear at his door. The hermit left what was going to be mine, mine, to his granddaughter. Fabiana broke my son's heart when she left for Rio. She hasn't done one thing to improve the property."

Prestle was gazing out of the window, twirling his reading eyeglasses on his finger.

"Hey, I'm talking to you."

"I hear you. Those birds are distracting."

Glorieta glanced toward the noisy birds and dismissed them as unimportant. "Anyway, I deserved that property. After all, I put up with that grouch for a whole month before he died. Then, that brat girl comes to visit him, and on his deathbed, he determines that the land will be hers when she marries. It's a travesty, isn't it, Prestle?" She put her glass on his desk.

"More?" he asked. Glorieta nodded. Prestle handed her another glass of whisky. She gulped it, contorted her face, and continued, "Monlevade was going to buy it and ... never mind. He intended to transform the ranch into a resort." She put the glass on Prestle's desk. Imagining herself as a pioneer on top of a mountain placing a waving flag on the ranch, she said, "The land is mine. And Prestle, I have a plan."

"What do you have in mind, my Glo?"

"My son. Fabiana broke up with him when she went to study tourism or whatever in Rio. If she ever comes back, I want them to get back together. And you will help me."

"How?"

"I'm thinking. I'll let you know soon."

"Come here, my Glo. Show me the new things you bought at the mall."

"When I saw your generous deposit in my account, I said to myself, I must reward you, darling." She unbuttoned her silk blouse to show off her new lace bra and pointed to herself like a game show host, revealing a prize, "This is not all. Smell this." Prestle sniffed her neck. "Oh, Glo, you have good taste and this perfume is so, so..."

"So-so? It's very expensive, you know. Do you like it or not?"

"I do. I, I ..." Prestle felt shortness of breath and sat down.

"Oh, no, no, no." She buttoned her shirt and called Prestle's secretary, who came in and took a blood pressure monitor from the septuagenarian's desk drawer. She took his pressure.

"It's all good, you hear me, Mr. Prestle? Drink more fluids. You are fine, you hear me?" His secretary said, tapping his hand. She put the monitor back in the drawer and left.

"More fluids, huh? Wanna whisky?" Glorieta teased suggestively.

He nodded in complicity.

"Prestle! Stop scaring me. You are fine. I'm leaving now. Where are the blueprints?"

"What blueprints?"

"Monlevade's. I left them on your desk."

Prestle shook his head. "Ask your secretary then, *criatur…*" Glorieta's pitch was a notch higher; she caught herself before calling him *criatura,* a term that she used to call anyone who annoyed her. He obliged and his secretary said she was not aware of any blueprint.

"We need to find them."

Glorieta massaged her head, stomped out in her high heels, and rushed to her car in the bank's parking garage.

As always, Glorieta found no parking in front of her house. She parked a block away and stayed inside the vehicle, screaming, "Argh! Where is that tube?" She retraced her memory. "The day after Monlevade gave me the tube, I brought it to the bank, put it on Prestle's desk… Prestle wasn't feeling good, so I left... If not there, then it's still in my bedroom."

She got out of the car and fanned herself. "This heat...I hate it!" Distracted, her high heel got caught on the cracks on the sidewalk. Pulling it free, she marched home, went to her bedroom, and stood at the door, ready to attack. Ceeda was hanging clothes in the closet. "Out, *criatura*! How many times do I have to ask you not to enter my bedroom when I'm not in?" Apologizing, Ceeda laid the rest of the clothes on the bed and slipped out of the room.

Glorieta slammed the door shut. She bent her knees to look under the bed. She tore through her closet and drawers, careless of the clothes that fell to the floor, and cursed. Sighing, she sat up on her bed and grabbed the box of chocolate kept in the drawer of her night table.

There was a knock at the door.

"What do you want?"

"Mom?" Johnny said, opening the door and gazing at the messy room.

"Leave me alone," she said. Johnny nodded and closed the door.

"Monlevade, why did you have to die and leave me in the cold?" Glorieta whined before stuffing her mouth with bonbons and throwing the wrappings on the floor. She then threw the empty box and screamed, "Stupid Fabiana! You'll pay me dearly. Oh, you will."

Johnny entered the dining room as Ceeda was bringing the mashed potato tray to the table. "You made me my favorite. Thank you. You are the best cook. I don't know what's eating my mom. But I tell you, Tornado Glorieta is back!"

Ceeda placed a tray of mashed potatoes on the table. Even before tasting it, Johnny said, "So delicious! Mom's loss. Ceeda, you are the best!"

"Nah! I'm just happy to cook for you. You are a good person." Ceeda leaned closer and whispered, "Unlike your mother." Johnny nodded and smiled in complicity.

"I think I know why Mom is mad today," he said.

"Huh, Isn't she mad every day?" Ceeda said.

***

Earlier at the bank, Prestle had asked everyone if they had seen a Sandy Lagoons tube filled with blueprints.

Johnny had seen his mother bring the tube into the conference room a few days ago. When he noticed the Rancho Santa Fabiana label, he secreted the blueprints on his desk.

Now, they were hidden in his room. A slow smile worked across his face. He took another spoonful of Ceeda's luscious mashed potatoes. *So Fabiana is coming back to build a resort.* He clasped his hands in anticipation.

After dinner, curiosity got the better of Johnny. He knocked and opened his mother's door just a crack. Glancing at the messy bedroom, he intended to ask, "Looking for a tube?" But the box of chocolate on Glorieta's lap distracted him. "May I have candy?" Glorieta threw the entire box at the door. "Go away. And do yourself a favor. Go look at your bulging belly in the mirror."

Johnny sighed and went to his room. He lay on his bed staring at the ceiling. When he was eight years old, he discovered a box of chocolate carelessly discarded on his mother's night table. Glorieta walked in and caught Johnny red-handed. "Do you want to become an elephant?"

Johnny jumped and turned around in fright. The half-eaten chocolate was still in his dirty fingers. Sheepishly, he mumbled that he wanted to be a jaguar.

Glorieta pushed him towards Ceeda, who was hovering in the doorway. "Don't be fresh with me. I'll wash your mouth with soap." Ceeda took Johnny's hand and, as soon as they were out of earshot, whispered in his ears, "Come, let's play outside; you can be my little jaguar."

***

It was New Year's Eve. Looking at her wristwatch, Fabiana said, "9 PM. Still early, I'll call him one more time. What have I got to lose?" She walked to the nearest phone booth and engaged in a mental conversation with him. *Oh! Paolo, so nice to hear your voice. Of course, I'll go to the Reveillon tonight with you. What color will you wear? I don't know if you know about a fun New Year's Eve Brazilian tradition. If you wear a yellow outfit, it means you want to attract money. Red, passion. White, peace. Green, good health. Me? Do you want me to surprise you?* Fabiana heard the coins drop and the dial tone and hesitated. 'I'm in the mood for romance. No! I won't mention any of the colors. My red outfit could backfire on me. He could run the other way!' The phone call once again went unanswered.

Back at her place, Fabiana passed by the landlord slumped on the couch, drinking from a bottle of champagne. When he saw her, he slurred what sounded like a Happy New Year.

Fabiana darted to her bedroom, locked the door, and spent the last day of the year tossing in bed and hugging her pillow. She made two resolutions.

A new place by the beach and reconnection with Paolo. The second one put a smile on her face. She gave a huge sigh of relief, convincing herself that counselor Janice would know more about Paolo's whereabouts. Fabiana could hardly wait for school to resume.

The morning sun was gleaming off the shiny percussion instruments, blasting samba music on several streets in Rio de Janeiro announcing the upcoming pre-carnival festivities. All modes of transportation were taking longer due to the several detours along the way.

Fabiana rode the bus on her way to the institute, sighing. Occupying the first seat, diagonally to the driver, she could see joy on the faces of kids and adults crowding the streets, sweating from dancing as if nobody was looking, swaying their arms in the air, jumping up and down, marching, clapping hands, and singing at the top of their lungs. Still longing for Paolo, Fabiana didn't share the festive energy in the air.

At the door of counselor Janice's office, Fabiana hesitated. The deafening sound of the massive drums, still reverberating in her ears, merged with the sound of the pounding telex machine.

"The list of the chosen ones is in," announced counselor Janice, smartly dressed in a navy blue skirt suit. She stood by the Siemens telex machine, watching it noisily type the graduates' names being offered an internship at the institute's network of tourism organizations.

Upon detaching the list from the machine, she waved the document in the air and turned to the group of graduates quickly gathering in her office. "If your name is here, congratulations. If it's not listed, don't be discouraged. Please apply again and check back next month. I guarantee our network will choose you next time." Leaving her office towards the long corridor, she was followed by the excited and hopeful students. Clara hurried to join the group.

Janice's employee I.D. card with her smiling photo above the name dangled from her collar, swinging side to side as she passed by a series of idyllic posters depicting global destinations.

Upon reaching and unlocking a glass case on the wall, she removed last month's list and affixed the newest one. The list contained three columns - the soon-to-be graduate's name, department, and tour company. Then, she locked the glass case and proceeded to return to her office. She passed by and smiled at Fabiana and Clara who were waiting for their turn to stand in front of the bulletin board. The two girls were wearing metallic jeans and t-shirts with the *I LOVE RIO* slogan. Counselor Janice stopped walking and looked at the giggling girls, making way to see the list.

"Yes! I can't believe I got it. Marketing Department Intern, Embratur." Clara turned and saw Janice a few feet away, looking at them. Smiling, she gave the counselor two thumbs up. Then she turned to Fabiana, who was still reading the list.

It was in alphabetical order of first names. Fabiana was hoping that her name somehow had got misspelled or misplaced and was reading the entire list. Sighing, she said, "I'm happy for you, Clara."

"Sorry, Fabiana." Clara put her hand on Fabiana's shoulders. "But, I'll tell you this. Once I'm in and running the entire tourism agency, I'll offer you a great position in the company. Deal?"

Counselor Janice overheard Fabiana say, "The institute guarantees a job to all students. Why didn't I get any assignment?"

Counselor Janice asked Fabiana to follow her to her office. She shifted some papers on her desk and held a telephone message from her While You Were Out pile. "This request arrived this morning. I think you are the ideal candidate. Driving for –"

"Sorry, I don't want to be rude, but I didn't invest all this money to be a dri-"

"- at Rio by Night tours."

The image of Paolo's business card flashed in her mind. Fabiana asked, "Starting when?"

"Tonight."

Fabiana hoped her excitement wasn't too obvious. Her disappointment when she discovered the Institute hadn't found her a lucrative tourism position couldn't suppress her anticipation of seeing Paolo again. She was positive the attraction had been mutual.

Tonight, she would find out exactly where they stood. Fabiana finished signing her employment papers and told Clara she would be waiting for her outside.

The relentless sunshine forced Fabiana to stay inside the nearby phone booth. Since she was there, she decided to place a long-distance call to her mother in Jungle City.

Pearl grew her own vegetables. With doting eyes, she examined a dozen sweet potatoes suspended by toothpicks in plastic containers of water and was about to refresh the water when a ringing telephone interrupted her. She placed the watering can on the floor of the back porch, dried her hands on a kitchen towel, and went to the living room to answer it. Her face opened up in a smile at the sound of Fabiana's voice.

"Mom," Fabiana said. "What's new?"

After the usual greetings, Pearl said, "We've got new neighbors, Ula and her two kids. The daughter, Carole, is about your age. I offered her a prep job, cutting onions. She only lasted a couple of days. Wouldn't keep her tears out of the onions. I let her brother, Nico, deliver the orders for a few days. Had to fire him after he arrived drunk one morning."

"Mom, be very careful with drunk people. I just called to say hello to you and Manuelito. How is he doing?"

"Your brother is doing good. Every day he wears the *I Love Rio* baseball cap you sent him. He's a sweetheart, stepping in to help me after school, and I always worry about him when he drops off the orders to the clients under this torrent sun. The heat here is unbearable, as you know. We need rain. How are things at your end? Has the Institute placed you?"

Fabiana sensed the apprehension behind her mother's question. Pearl couldn't afford even the modest monthly stipend she was spending on Fabiana's tuition. Fabiana dodged the question by announcing she had a gig for that evening, stressing it might lead to full-time employment. She quickly added that she was graduating this weekend. Pearl congratulated her and wished she and Manuelito could be there.

"No worries. I may not attend it myself."

Clara was approaching the phone booth, waving an envelope in the air.

"Oh, dear. I almost forgot. This is important. I don't want you to be alarmed..."

"Mom, what's the matter?"

"Well, a truck fell into the river near your property."

"A truck?"

"Yes, a tree-trimming truck. I have no idea what he was doing out there."

Clara waved the envelope impatiently.

"Sorry. I have to go. I'll deal with that situation when I come home. Have a great day, Mom. Keep cooking. You're the best. Love ya!" Fabiana exited the phone booth.

Pearl hung up the phone and returned to the porch where she finished refreshing the water of the sweet potatoes' containers.

"Counselor Janice asked me to give you this envelope," Clara said. "It's about your gig tonight."

Fabiana shoved the envelope into her backpack without opening it. "I hate driving."

"I don't blame you." Clara gave Fabiana a curious look. "I don't want to pry but I overheard you say something about going home. Are you planning to leave after graduation?"

"Who knows?" Fabiana sighed, glancing at her watch. "Where does the time go? I gotta be at Rio by Night offices by 5:30."

"Plenty of time," Clara said. If we happen to bump into any samba street parties, let's do like everybody does."

"Do what?"

Swinging her arms at the rhythm of a carnival tune, Clara sang, "We join the party. Deal?"

The girls laughed and walked towards Clara's car, parked in front of a bathing suit store. The swimsuit in the window caught Fabiana's eyes immediately. The material featured a feline pattern.

"Wait here." Fabiana hurried into the store and bought the bathing suit without trying it on. She rejoined Clara with naughty eyes shoving the shopping bag in her backpack. "One day, this is going to be for Paolo's eyes only." They giggled, and then Fabiana tapped her watch and said. "I'm going to be late. He must be waiting for me."

The Tour and the Longing

Fabiana found the guy bent over, looking for something under the Rio by Night Tours Volkswagen Kombi van. She smiled and said, "Hello, stranger. I'll be your driver tonight."

"Great. Thanks for coming on such short notice." The man straightened and turned out to be short and blond.

Fabiana tried to hide her disappointment. "I'm... Fabiana from the Institute."

"Greg, the owner of Rio by Night Tours." He handed her a package. "Please wear this Polo shirt over your top, and let's go. Shall we? Wait a sec. There's my pen." He bent to pick it up under the van.

Fabiana took a deep breath, "I might need some help with all the detour signs, okay?" She started around the van to the driver's seat.

Reading a list of names on his clipboard, Greg didn't seem to hear her question. "On second thought, my voice is very hoarse today. I'll drive. You'll do the talking." He gave her a script and motioned her to climb into the seat in the back.

She intended to inquire about Paolo's whereabouts but ended up asking, "Where to?"

Greg's lack of response left her wondering whether his hearing was as bad as his voice. *Everything will be fine,* she thought while looking at Greg's image in the rearview mirror. His furrowed brows made him look angry.

Many streets on the way to the Copacabana Palace Hotel were closed due to pre-carnival festivities. Celebrants of all ages followed the percussionists, singing and dancing any way they pleased.

The sun gleamed off the shiny percussion instruments, blasting samba music momentarily blinding Fabiana. Greg quickly put on his sunglasses, and Fabiana used the script as a shield.

Greg's demeanor improved the moment he pulled up at the hotel. He jumped out with a big grin and welcomed three middle-aged couples from Italy wearing matching green t-shirts and an attractive woman in her fifties wearing a pink rhinestone baseball cap.

Fabiana hadn't finished going over the script. She took a deep breath. *Dear Lord, here we go.*

Greg opened the van doors, motioning for the couples to take the middle and back seats. Fabiana wondered where the solo woman was going to sit. Much to her surprise, Greg asked the American woman to squeeze in between Fabiana and him on the front seat.

Fabiana kneeled on the crowded seat to face the group. She welcomed them, introducing the driver and herself, "I'll be your guide tonight," she gulped. Glancing at the script written in several languages, Fabiana read the English paragraph "Copacabana is famous for its sidewalk. The black and white wave mosaic represents the Amazon river. Architect Roberto Burle Max designed it in 1970." Then, she mentally thanked her Italian language training at the Institute and repeated it in broken Italian. The group turned to observe the pavement but their eyes lingered on the sun-bathers who in all sorts of bathing suits, were either walking, playing volleyball, practicing cooper, or simply worshiping the sun on the sands of the Atlantic Ocean.

Greg drove on. Fabiana prayed, *Oh dear Lord, let me sound interesting.* "We are leaving Copacabana and entering Ipanema. There's a famous restaurant at the corner of this street." She pointed out a rustic restaurant with outdoor seating. "Garota de Ipanema Restaurant. Tom Jobim and Vinicius de Moraes wrote the song, initially called *The Girl Who Passes By*. The song was later renamed *The Girl from Ipanema*."

Greg pressed a button on the dashboard, and the song began playing. *Tall and tan and young and lovely...* The Italians hummed along. The American woman sang and altered the lyrics, "the boy from Ipanema saw me and then he said his heart belonged to me." Holding back a laugh, Greg and Fabiana looked at each other.

Several blocks ahead, Fabiana read, "Next on our agenda is the Leblon neighborhood. Great for surfing. Do any of you know how to surf?" The Italians conferred among themselves, "Navigare? Si, si." The American pouted her lips and muttered, "Your other tour guide promised to teach me. I can't get a hold of him. I thought he'd be back from the U.S. by now." Fabiana looked out the window. *Is she talking about Paolo? No wonder he's never returned my calls.*

"*Carnavale?*" One of the Italians asked. "*Quando è il carnevale?*"

"Find the part referring to Mardi Gras," Greg suggested. "This year's Carnavale is from March 2nd to Ash Wednesday, March 7th," Fabiana read.

"Will Paolo be back in time to see the Parade?" the woman asked.

What does this woman want with Paolo? Fabiana felt a flush of red hit her cheek. Both women looked at Greg, eager for his reply. He shook his head. "Sorry, we're not allowed to give personal information about our employees."

The orange-brown shades of the sunset faded from the views of Sugarloaf mountain into a beautiful starry night. Greg maneuvered the vehicle around the many detours caused by the pre-carnival gatherings and stopped outside a nightclub. "We have arrived at Panorama Night Club for an authentic Brazilian dinner with a show."

"Don't bother reading the English text," the American woman drawled. "I've taken this tour with Paolo before."

Greg exited the van. Shaking his head, he walked around to open its doors. When everyone was outside, Fabiana approached Greg and whispered, "Now what?"

"Go and help the group settle in. The reservation is under the company name. We wait out here. I've seen this show too many times."

"I get it. No problem. I'm not hungry anyway," Fabiana said, relaxing her shoulders. "I'll be right back."

After the group had been seated, Fabiana returned to the parking lot. She opened the back door, "Greg, are you okay?"

He brought his hands towards his ears. "My head is spinning, and my voice is getting hoarser by the minute. I … I'm going to take a nap if it's alright."

"That woman was talking about a previous guide, right?"

"She's a stalker...she's been on three of our tours looking for Paolo."

"Is he all right?"

"Who?"

"This Paolo," she said, trying to sound nonchalant.

"I guess. He's been transferred to the Pantanal. Now, please close the door. Let me sleep."

Three and a half hours later, the tourists returned to the van with *glow*ing smiles. "How was it?" Fabiana asked while the group took their seats. They took turns raving about the food and the show, from *"Buonissimo, Maraviglioso"* to *"Pio Bello."* The American, wearing her rhinestone cap backward, looked spent. After distributing water to all, Greg started the drive back to the Copacabana Palace Hotel.

The American started sliding down towards Fabiana. "Cocabacan–," she mumbled. "How do you say it?"

Fabiana gently straightened the woman and rolled her eyes. *Didn't Paolo teach you how to say it?* "Like the song, *Copacabana.* You know, by Barry Manilow."

Greg made a U-Turn and began heading toward the hotel. They all sat in silence as the engine hummed. The drivers around them seemed in a hurry, but not Greg. He was one of the most passive drivers ever. Later, when he pulled up to the hotel entrance, Greg and Fabiana exited the car, with Greg going around the van.

"Here we are," Fabiana said. "Any questions? I'll be happy to answer."

"Do you know how to get a hold of Paolo?"

Fabiana glanced at Greg, who subtly rolled his eyes and shook his head.

Greg helped the tourists exit the van, saying, "Please make sure to take all your belongings with you." The Italians were visibly happy. They tipped Fabiana and said, *"Grazie tanto."* The American produced a business card. She kissed the card, gave it to Greg, and said loud enough for Fabiana to hear, "If you hear from Paolo, this card is for him." It was Fabiana's turn to roll her eyes.

Moments later, Greg reached for the glove compartment and retrieved a plastic envelope. It fell at Fabiana's feet. As she bent to pick it up, she noticed Paolo's employee ID card. Paolo stared at Fabiana from his ID, or so she thought.

Greg walked her to the sidewalk and hailed a cab. "The institute will pay you."

Departures and Discoveries

At home, Fabiana stepped into the living room and turned the light on. Her gaze drifted from the wall clock, displaying 1:12 a.m., to a body wrapped from head to toe in a light soft linen sheet, snoring on the couch. As she passed by the couch, the person turned onto his side, leaving the back of his head visible. Glancing at the bald spot and ponytail, Fabiana raised an eyebrow. *The landlord? Now he's drinking to the point of falling asleep on the sofa? My goodness, I gotta get out of here as soon as possible.* Turning the light off, she went to her bedroom and locked the door.

A note from the landlord lay on top of her pillow. After reading it, she pulled her empty suitcase off the closet shelf and left it, opened, on the floor by her backpack. Sighing, she laid down without changing into her pajamas.

Several times during the night, images of the Rhinestoned cowgirl and Paolo's ID card filled her mind. "Why do I even bother with Paolo?" hugging her pillow, she closed her eyes.

Bright sunlight filtered through the curtains, announcing the new day. Yawning, Fabiana lifted the cotton sheet that half-covered her body, stretched, got up, and opened her backpack. The sexy bathing suit bought the day before was among notebooks, books, and her wallet. She changed into it, wrapped her body in the matching beach wrap, and admired her image in the closet mirror. "Paolo, do you deserve this? I wanted to show it to you so much. Now, I don't know."

The cool morning breeze reached her skin like a wave from the ocean, making goosebumps rise on her bare arms. "For your eyes only, Paolo." In her mind, she could see Paolo's eyes transfixed with desire.

Suddenly, she heard someone stepping on dried leaves outside. She looked through the window in time to see the back of the guy with a ponytail and bald spot in a sleeveless t-shirt, like the landlord leaving the premises. His note and possible peeping made it easier for her to spring into action.

After showering and changing into her jeans and T-shirt, Fabiana packed her belongings, grabbed her make-up case, and entered the living room, holding her backpack in front of her as a shield. She approached the landlord, who was reading the paper.

"I got your note and I'll be leaving today."

"Yeah! Just pay me for last week. I've got my family coming over the holidays, and they need the room. In fact, one arrived last night."

Fabiana reached into her purse and handed him the money. The front door opened. A man with a ponytail let himself in and smiled, revealing sharp canine teeth. The landlord held out his hand, "My twin brother." Frowning, Fabiana thought, *Dracula, both of you* and rushed outside.

She hailed a cab to the nearest travel agency and booked her return ticket to Jungle City. Her next stop was a hotel in Botafogo Beach, where she booked a room facing Corcovado Mountain. She phoned her friend Clara. "Guess where I am?.... No, in a hotel, I can see Christ the Redeemer looking at me... I'm going home...Mom needs help with her business... Leaving in two days...The gig? ... I'll meet you at the institute this afternoon and tell you all about it."

After signing papers in counselor Janice's office, Fabiana found Clara in the student lounge.

"So my friend," Clara said, "Tell me all about last night. How did it go with Paolo?"

Fabiana relayed her disappointment, the annoying Rhinestoned cowgirl, the uninspiring script, and the landlord's note. "But enough about me, I have something for you." Fabiana handed Clara a bag containing her collection of scented bubble bath soap, a few unopened cereal boxes, and several canned foods.

"Thank you so much, Fabiana. I'm sad to see you go. Let me give you a ride to the airport."

***

Fabiana called her mother from the hotel and was reminded that Rancho Santa Fabiana was in a dire state of abandonment. "I'll sell it, Mom."

Following the call, Fabiana crossed the street and walked along the beach. Her modest swim dress made her feel self-conscious. From behind her cat-eye sunglasses, she discreetly observed men and women of all sizes and shapes parade down the beach in tiny bathing suits.

Two days later, on the way to the Santos Dumont Airport, Clara said, "I really wish you could stay for graduation and carnival."

"I'm not in the mood for carnival this year. Thanks, anyway."

At the departure terminal, the girls hugged tightly.

Fabiana proceeded to the gate and hopped on her VARIG flight to Campo Grande. After fastening her seat belt, she leafed through the airline magazine. A picture of feline eyes grabbed her attention. The jaguar's eyes morphed into Paolo's eyes. Each set of amber eyes awoke feelings inside her. While Paolo's brought her warm feelings, the jaguar's intense gaze coupled with a hissing sound like a machine sawing wood, scared her. Opening her eyes, Fabiana realized that the noise she just heard was the screeching sound of the airplane landing in Campo Grande.

A one-hour cab ride brought Fabiana to the bus station. At the ticket window, she learned that the bus ride to Jungle City had been canceled for the day due to maintenance. She sat down, trying to decide where to spend the night. Fabiana phoned Madame Sophia and was relieved to be invited to spend the night.

Fabiana went around the back of the house as instructed and found not only the door unlocked but also a white cat meowing in a manner that indicated it wanted to get in. Fabiana entered the kitchen, followed by the cat. She found an empty jar lid inside the sink. She wanted to fill it with milk, but feeling she was not at liberty to open the refrigerator, filled it with water and left it on the floor. The cat disappeared inside the house.

Fabiana went to the living room. The darkness created by heavy brown curtains contrasted with the brightness of the kitchen. She left her suitcase by the door and sat down on the tattered couch.

After a few minutes, Sophia opened the door and waved goodbye to the client who was leaving. She brushed her hand on her long skirt and opened her arms for a hug. Fabiana stood up and said, "Sophia, thank you, thank you. It's very nice of you to let me stay."

"My dear Fabiana." The seventy-year-old woman fixed her signature Sophia Loren eyeglasses on the bridge of her nose. "How time flies. Last time I saw you, you were, what, thirteen?"

Fabiana nodded. "1977, after my grandfather died."

"May he rest in peace. How about something to drink?"

"I'm fine. How about I take you out for dinner — my treat."

Sophia accepted the offer.

"I wonder if I could bother you with another favor," Fabiana continued.

"A manicure?" Sophia laughed and looked at Fabiana's fingernails. "But let me tell ya, your nails are fine, dear. So, I shall apply my new decals. Would you like that? By the way, I think you'll like my new roaring jaguar."

"No way! A roaring jaguar?" Fabiana repeated with an amused look on her face.

"Come and see what I mean," Sophia clapped her hands in delight, but Fabiana was repelled by the chubby woman's long curved nails that reminded her of vulture talon. The middle-aged woman motioned from the door of the manicure room. "After you, dear."

She directed Fabiana's attention to a metal jaguar head, no bigger than a coffee mug, on the corner of the manicure table. "I got this music box a long time ago. Cute, ya? It needs to be wound with tender, loving care. Please sit down and watch it roar."

Fabiana thought that the jaguar sounded like a bad carburetor. It emitted several jerky choking noises, then died.

"I assure you. This really is a conversation piece." Sophia slapped it gently and moved it closer to Fabiana.

Fabiana turned the winding key and it came loose. "So sorry, so very sorry."

"No worries, dear. Watch what I'm going to do." Sophia stuffed the jaguar's open mouth with a few incense sticks and lit them.

The incense smoke drifted toward Fabiana. She held her breath momentarily, *Gosh! What kind of burning incense is this?*

Sophia sat down and reached for a box of nail polish bottles under the table. She started painting the nails. "What is it that is bothering you, child?" She studied the pensive girl over the rim of her large eyeglasses.

"Will I find another jaguar to replace this one that I broke?"

"Don't be silly! I can read people. Good things are coming your way, but you must go over some unfinished business in Jungle City."

"I think I know what you mean."

"Good. I'm sure you do." Madame Sophia sighed.

Fabiana was surprised by the quickness of the nail polish application. "Madame Sophia, thank you. I'll be glad to pay you for your time and get you another music box. Just let me know where to find one." When the nails dried, Fabiana massaged her temples. The incense was overpowering and giving her a headache.

"Now that the nails are dry, the decals. I got these from a well-traveled client." Sophia applied animal print decals on Fabiana's nails.

"Fabulous," said Fabiana, admiring her nails.

"Now, come with me." Sophia led Fabiana down a hall leading to three closed doors. "Bathroom, my bedroom, and the guest, I mean, your bedroom tonight."

Fabiana gazed at the black and white photos adorning the corridor wall, pointing out toward a picture.

Sophia explained, "Oh, that's me in this *Simca Chambord* car ad. Large as a boat. Green pistachio color. Beautiful cream color interior. My fiancé, a big shot, set up this opportunity for me. It was around the late fifties or could it be the late sixties? Anyway, I was beautiful back then. Little did I know it would be my last gig. One day, out of the blue, my fiancé left me. No one has since hired me. Over these past years, I had my share of ups and downs. And I've never had another meaningful relationship since".

"So sorry to hear about that," Fabiana said.

Madame Sophia asked if Fabiana wanted tea or something, and Fabiana said she was fine. They sat down on the couch to watch tv and continued talking about themselves.

"Do you like reading?"

Fabiana nodded and added, "Machado de Assis is my favorite author."

"I read his *Bras Cubas* and *Dom Casmurro* in high school. What do you like about him?"

"I like that he writes about the contradictions of society in a very realistic way, "Fabiana said. "His novels generally depict jealousy, paranoia, and adultery. I don't know about you, but I have always kept thinking about his wonderful characters long after the story was over. Did you know he taught himself later in life to speak French, English, German and Greek? I'll be happy learning English well, but I'll truly need a tutor. How about you? What do you read?"

"Anything related to new age topics or the cartoons. I don't buy books. I stop once in a while at the library a few blocks from here." Madame Sophia shrugged before replying.

"My, my former boyfriend also reads cartoons. He's nice. But I'm not ready to settle down and start a family. We've known each other since 1977, the year my grandpa died," Fabiana blabbered. She immediately realized the unsolicited comment she made.

"What does he do?"

"He works for a bank, lending money to small businesspeople like my mother."

Fabiana nodded and looked at another framed photograph on the wall.

"Wonderful, isn't it? A gift from a friend."

"Wow! He captured the jaguar's rosette spots very well. I had a close encounter with a jaguar once. Its spots really resembled roses. You know what? About unfinished business, I think you were referring to my artwork. I used to be an illustrator. Maybe I should pick that up again. I'll draw something for you."

"Don't worry, dear," they went into the kitchen, where they heard a howling sound.

"By the way, that reminds me," Fabiana said, "I let your cat in."

"A cat? I don't have one."

"I thought it was yours."

"No, not mine." Guided by the howling sound, Sophia opened the cabinet under the sink.

"Oh, hello there. Looking for something to eat under my sink?"

"Speaking about eating, where can I take you out for dinner?"

"There's this nice Italian restaurant called Primavera, about a fifteen-minute walk from here. We can go after my 4 o'clock client. If you are hungry now, I could make you a tuna sandwich?"

"No thanks. I had something to eat at the bus station. I'm going to take a walk on the main street to pass the time."

After Fabiana left, Sophia squatted and stared at the hunched cat. "Are you arthritic like me? Yah? Well, don't expect me to take care of you. Out." The cat didn't move. Fearless, Sophia rested her hand on the back of its neck and grasped the loose skin. Carrying the cat at arm's length, she opened the front door and looked in all directions. The street was deserted. Certain that no one was looking, she abandoned the cat at a nearby ravine. Then, rolling eyes and whistling a happy tune, she wiped her hands on her long skirt and returned home.

Fabiana leisurely strolled past the stores on the streets near Sophia's house. Her eye was caught by a pair of creepy sandals on a mannequin. The fake snakehead with its forked tongue on the toe looked very real. It had an adjustable ankle wrap stretching up to the mannequin's knee. The four-inch heels were quite different from the tennis shoes and flats Fabiana usually wore. A saleslady, propped at the entrance of the store, asked Fabiana if she wanted to try them on. Enticed, Fabiana followed her inside and took a seat.

When the saleslady opened the box, she gave Fabiana the sandals as if they were precious pieces of art. Laughing, Fabiana played with the forked snake tongue.

She rolled the legs of her trousers up to her knees and slipped her feet into the sandals. "They fit like a glove," Fabiana admired her legs in the mirror. The other salespeople nodded at Fabiana in delightful agreement. Fabiana bought the snake stilettos but once she left the store, she fought a little bit of buyer's remorse. *Where am I going to wear my brand-new high heels?*

Fabiana passed by a perfume kiosk on the sidewalk and allowed the salesperson to spritz different perfume testers on her forearm, hands, and wrists. She inquired about a few international brands, smelled them, and, praying that they were not fakes, bought two scents as gifts.

Strings of Fate

Fabiana returned to Sophia's house a little after 4 PM, took a shower, and rested in her room. A couple of hours later, Sophia knocked at the door and announced she was ready. They walked to Primavera restaurant and were the only guests there at that time.

"Food is good here," Sophia said and ordered two cocktails called jaguar milk. Soon, she was sipping hers like a connoisseur. She motioned Fabiana to drink too.

Fabiana obliged. "Strong for my taste. Made with sugar cane alcohol, right?"

"Yes, it's an acquired taste, dear. I was on a jungle safari the first time I tried one."

"When was that?"

"1972. It was beautiful. I was in love." Sophia gulped her drink. "What's love anyway, heh?" She answered her own question. "Allowing another person to take your everything away. Has that ever happened to you?"

Fabiana thought of her limited romantic experience and confided, "Maybe once or twice."

The waiter brought bread and took their orders– spaghetti with meatballs, lasagna, and another jaguar milk for Sophia.

"Some people treat some people better than others," Sophia said, drinking her second cocktail as if it were water.

The jaguar milk was making Fabiana dizzy. Her face was burning. She ate a piece of bread. "You could say that of my late grandfather. You knew him. Am I not right?"

"Indeed, dear. The nicest person on earth, he was. He liked to do things his way."

Sophia called the waiter and ordered a third jaguar milk for herself.

Fabiana raised her cocktail, "Cheers to good people."

When dinner was over, and the bill was on the table, Sophia reached in slow motion for something in her purse. Fabiana raised her hands, "Sophia, I insist. Dinner is on me."

"I know, dear. I just wanted to show you this." Sophia pulled out a set of business cards bundled with an elastic band. Fabiana watched her with curiosity.

Sophia laid the business cards on the table as if she were preparing to tell a fortune. "Aha! Here it is." She picked up a card and gave it to Fabiana.

"Trevor, P.I.?"

"Trevor is a friend who lives near you. You never know when you'll need a private investigator. Please stop by and say that I send regards."

In the morning, Fabiana gifted one of the perfume bottles to Sophia and proceeded to the sidewalk to wait for the cab to take her to the bus station. Sophia remained standing by the red bougainvillea gracing the façade of her house until the cab disappeared from her view.

Sophia dialed a number. "Guess who was here? ... That clueless girl! ... She's going back there. ... I know. It works in our favor. ... In the meantime, don't you screw up this time!" Sophia hung up the phone.

Examining her fingernails, Sophia asked herself, "How do you want your nails today, dear?" After a few seconds, changing into an authoritative voice, she replied to herself, "I want a French manicure with black tips."

Fabiana left Madame Sophia's house and headed to the bus station, immersed in frustrating thoughts. She had lost Paolo. It dawned on her that she had convinced herself of being head over heels in love with Paolo. The swimsuit with rosette pattern she had bought before her tour gig in Rio, intended solely for his eyes, only intensified her growing sense of disillusionment.

Worried about her mother's disapproval of the skimpy swimsuit, Fabiana discreetly disposed of the swimsuit in the trash bin at the Campo Grande bus station, hoping to leave behind not just the tangible reminder but also the unfulfilled expectations that had burdened her heart.

She boarded the bus, reread the heartfelt letter she had written to Paolo after their second date in Rio, the one kept in her makeup case. The six-hour journey from Campo Grande to Jungle City was dull, and Fabiana dozed off. When she woke up in the morning, annoyed, she ripped the letter to shreds and tossed the pieces into the nearest trash bin as she stepped off the bus, heading for the cab line.

***

Flaky Candy and Second Chances

Upon learning from the bank receptionist that Fabiana had returned to town, Johnny became uneasy. His response to anxiety involved eating peanut candies that triggered memories from his tenth birthday party.

Gazing out his office window without seeing the luxurious forest, including pink trumpet, jacaranda, and palm trees, the only thing on Johnny's mind was Fabiana. He sat down, leaned back on his seat, read a few documents, tossed them on top of his desk, and opened a drawer, and his eyes fell on a flaky peanut candy bar box.

Johnny did not need to read the nutrition information. The scars of his tenth birthday party flashed in his mind. His sole guest, a boy next door, had gifted him a box of these bars. After the party, Johnny sat on the porch and gobbled all ten bars, leaving none for his mother. Glorieta grabbed the box from his lap, shoved it in his face, and forced him to read it. One-hundred-and-fifteen calories. Each bar!

Every time he looked at the box, the word 'each' echoed in his mind. The wrapped bars were half the size of a business card.

Shrugging, Johnny took one out, unwrapped it, and ate it with delight. He tapped his rounded belly and took another one, yet another one, and in less than two minutes, he had eaten 6 bars. Still chewing, he unwrapped the seventh peanut bar and jumped when the intercom buzzed. He lifted the phone, tried to swallow, and mumbled, "Hell…hello." Like a bird, he moved his head up and down as he listened to the voice on the other side of the line. "Wait a minute," he managed to say. He poured himself a glass of water and finally swallowed the flaky candy. It was his secretary saying his 2 PM client had canceled.

Johnny hung up the phone, shook his head, and took the last two flaky peanut bars. He ate both at one time. He put all the candy wrappers in the pocket of his trousers and stepped out of his office determined to drive to Fabiana's place.

Fabiana was in her backyard studio, holding a drawing of Johnny's eyes. When Johnny knocked on the barn door, she opened it, looked up from her sketch and gazed at Johnny's eyes right in front of her.

"Bee! I missed you."

"Johnny. How's it going?"

"All is good. You look good. Do you have plans for the carnival?"

"No. I need peace and quiet."

"You just read my mind." He loosened his tie. "Hot in here, isn't it? Would you care for ice cream?"

Fabiana relented. They went to the only ice cream parlor in the city. Nothing had changed. The birds, the beautiful pink trumpet trees, and even the delicious acai ice cream that melted under the afternoon heat brought back memories and told Fabiana she was home.

On the way back, Johnny asked, "You completed your course?"

Fabiana nodded but that was it. She never apologized for leaving him so abruptly almost six months ago. Instead, she smiled and fanned herself.

"Looks like the air conditioning is out," he remarked, breaking the awkward silence in the car. Upon arriving back at her house, they exchanged a quick kiss. Johnny continued to stop by after work from that day on.

Fabiana's neighbor, Carole, had seen Johnny drive by her house several times. Tonight, she was waiting for him. She had donned tiny white shorts and a strapless white eyelet top over a fire engine red bra. She stood on the sidewalk by the iron gate, looking at her wristwatch, knowing he would admire her warm, brown skin and flashing eyes.

When Carole saw Johnny's car approaching, she locked eyes with the driver. That eye-gazing moment seemed like an eternity to both of them. The brief encounter was enough to lure Johnny to gaze through the rearview mirror to see the girl stretching her arms and bending to massage her calves. He almost drove past Fabiana's house.

***

After learning that Johnny and Fabiana were dating again, Glorieta had softened her approach to Johnny. She bought him a new shirt with a toucan pattern. "Wear this, Johnny. You gotta be a conquistador, a Casanova, ma boy. Ole'!" She said, pretending to play an invisible set of castanets. Glorieta poured a handful of the Brut cologne on her hands and approached him like a bull.

Zigzagging in front of his mother to avoid the cologne, Johnny dropped the box of chocolate he was planning to bring to Fabiana.

"Clumsy boy!" Glorieta snapped.

Johnny tried to make up for his avoidance maneuver. "This box of chocolate is for you, Mother." Leaving the box on the floor, Johnny stormed out of the house and drove to Fabiana's house, hoping to see the neighbor girl with the revealing top along the way.

***

Johnny stood behind Fabiana, watching her paint an eye on watercolor paper. Peeling a banana, he offered his unsolicited comments, "I don't get it. Why is the dead eye of a fish considered art?"

"Don't you have to go back to the bank?" Fabiana snapped and went outside for fresh air. She wished she could tell him that his eyes were the inspiration for her dead fish.

Johnny picked up the painting and carried it toward the door, studying it. At that exact moment, Fabiana opened the door to return to the room. The freshly painted artwork smashed against Johnny, smearing his polyester suit.

Fabiana stared at her ruined painting.

Johnny looked at the rainbow smear on the lapel of his suit and said, "You just ruined a perfect suit. What am I going to do?" He dropped the painting on the floor, looked at her with disappointment in his eyes, mumbled "Shit," and left.

Fabiana suppressed the urge to laugh. She looked through the window and went outside again. Tiny fruit flies were swarming around rotten banana peels, courtesy of Johnny. She grabbed the lid and slammed it on top of the trash can. She returned to her studio, looked at her damaged artwork, and decided to alter the subject. Using red and black pastel sticks, she turned the fisheye into a horrifying vision. The iris was red, and the eye was outlined in a thick black.

I'm getting tired of Johnny's tantrums. In fact, I don't know why I'm wasting my time with him. His behavior is ridiculous. "That's it. This is my last drawing of his eyes." Above all, Fabiana was not going to take Johnny's unfair and unsolicited criticism, either. "It's time for rosettes, once more."

"Johnny roars too much. If he thinks he is a jaguar, he isn't one to me." She shook her head. After drawing the jaguar's rosette spots, Fabiana took a deep breath and felt her frustration dissolve like ice under the sun.

Unexpected Neighbors

Pearl had come home in the afternoon. She was ready to return to her catering office when she saw Fabiana looking through the peephole.

"Who's out there?" she asked.

"Our new neighbor. What's her name?"

"Daughter or mother?" asked Pearl.

"The daughter."

"Carole," said Manuelito.

"It looks like she's been crying."

"Let her in," urged Pearl.

Fabiana opened the door at once. Carole entered, lowered her head, and wiped smudged mascara from under her eyes with her hands.

"Are you okay?" Pearl motioned the distraught girl to sit next to her. Carole obliged and broke into fresh tears.

"Manuelito, go get Carole a glass of water."

Manuelito promptly returned with a glass of cold water. Carole took a sip and returned the glass with shaking hands.

"You okay now?" Pearl asked. "What's the problem?"

"It's Nico! Didn't you hear the commotion in my house this morning?" Everyone shook their heads. Carole took a dirty tissue from under the sleeve of her top and timidly blew her nose. She folded the used tissue and put it back under her sleeve.

"Manuelito, Kleenex!" Fabiana shrieked. He quickly ran to the bathroom. When he returned, Pearl rolled her eyes, but Carole accepted the wad of toilet paper and blew her nose on it with gusto. After holding the wet toilet paper and glancing around uncertainty for a few seconds, Carole added it to the other tissues under her sleeve.

"This morning, we locked Nico in his room, from the outside, to prevent him from, uh --- okay, drinking." Carole looked at everybody and saw some puzzlement, but no one interrupted her.

"My brother is claustrophobic. He begged us to open it." Carole looked at Pearl with an expression of anguish.

"I see," Pearl nodded.

"So, my brother forced out the hinges, broke the door open, stormed out of the house in a terrible mood, and returned a few hours later. Crazy drunk. He started breaking things. Oh! Pearl. It was terrible! It was awful!"

"Did he hurt anybody?" asked Pearl.

"Oh no, he's never laid a finger on any of us." Carole sobbed and looked at Pearl. "Can I talk with you in private?"

"Mom," Fabiana interrupted. "I need to mail my curriculum vitae to the resorts in the area. Manuelito, can you give me a ride to the Post Office?"

Manuelito opened his hand and said, "For five dollars." Pearl rolled her eyes and gestured to Carole to follow her down the corridor. Pearl pulled the door closed behind them.

Once they were alone, Carole took a deep breath. "Pearl, Nico's not well. I need to borrow another one hundred, please."

Pearl hesitated. "Wait a minute. Borrow again? You promised to repay what I loaned you today."

"I was going to," Carole mumbled, holding a used tissue under her nose. "I want you to know that your kindness last month really helped all of us. But we need to refill Nico's meds. You are my last resort."

Pearl opened her purse and sternly said, "Fifty is all I have. I need to borrow money for my business."

With the money tightly folded in her closed hand, Carole followed Pearl back to the living room. Ignoring Fabiana and Manuelito, who were still negotiating the bike ride fare to the Post Office, Carole said, "Thank you for your kind understanding, Pearl. See you later."

Pearl said that she would be at her office finishing up the daily ledger and would be right back.

***

Johnny glanced through a brochure about making money by selling Tupperware. He tossed it and impatiently looked at the clock on the wall. It had advanced only five minutes from the last time he had checked it, 40 minutes before he could go to Fabiana's home. His eyes fell on his suit jacket stained with pastels from Fabiana's painting.

He closed the door of his office and went to the bathroom at the end of the corridor. Splashing water over the speckles of paint on his trousers only made the stain worse. "Damn. Half of my salary just went to waste." He recalled storming out of Fabiana's studio. "Who in their right mind would buy a painting of dead fish eyes? Art as I know it is the work of the grand master Botticelli."

When he returned, he saw the door was ajar. The chair where he'd draped his jacket had been swiveled. The person sitting on the chair turned towards him; Johnny's ruined jacket was on her lap.

"Mum?"

"No. The armadillo. What the heck happened to your jacket? Don't you know that you need to be presentable for the meeting?" his mother said irritably.

"What meeting?"

"We have an appointment to talk to your boss about your future here. Prestle is waiting. Come. Let's go." She stood up and tossed the damaged jacket carelessly on the chair. Pointing to the splash on Johnny's trouser belt area, she picked up the Tupperware brochure from the trash and said, "Here, cover your disgusting stain with this."

Glorieta did not knock at Prestle's door. She opened it and pulled her son inside. After Johnny awkwardly stepped in, Glorieta straightened her Prada suit and marched to a large armchair by the wall.

"Johnny!" Prestle was fixing his eyeglasses on his nose's bridge. "Please, take a seat, young man. How long have you been with us?" Johnny gingerly took the seat across from Prestle's desk, his back to his mother. Straightening his tie and resting the brochure on his tummy, Johnny said, "Two, no, almost three years."

Prestle looked past Johnny and glanced at Glorieta. She flirtatiously winked at him, flashing a sexy smile. Prestle smiled, and Johnny, thinking he was smiling at him, smiled back. Glorieta got up and stood by the side of Prestle's chair. She bit at the smudged orange lipstick and beamed at Johnny. It was time for Prestle to introduce Glorieta's idea to Johnny.

"Johnny, your scheme to save money on toilet paper was brilliant. An accomplishment worthy of a promotion. But we pride ourselves on being a family bank. You may have noticed that all our managers are married. And somehow, we, I mean the bank, has been waiting…" Prestle took his eyeglasses off and pretended to clean them. "...for you to let me know that the w-day has arrived."

"W-day?"

"Yes, win your promotion by tying the knots," explained Glorieta with confidence.

"Glorieta says you and Ms. Fabiana Grande are seeing one another again." Looking sternly into Johnny's eyes, he said, "Let us know when the W-day is." Prestle leaned back and fondled Glorieta's back, who cheered with laughter.

Johnny looked quizzically at his mother, who convincingly said, "Be a man with a plan, ma boy." Glorieta turned her attention to Prestle and said, "Let's drink. Cheers to the W-day!"

Johnny looked at his wristwatch, declined the drink, and respectfully said good-bye.

Prestle offered Glorieta a whisky on the rocks and asked, "So, my Glo, are you happy?"

Tapping her foot on the floor, showing some irritation, Glorieta shrugged, "I know my son. The brat won't follow through. Even if he marries Fabiana, he won't give me the satisfaction of getting a Power of Attorney. Oh! Prestle, I want Rancho Santa

Fabiana's deed into my name. I want Rancho Santa Fabiana's deed in my name.

"In 1977, when I took care of him, he agreed to leave his property to me. Granted, he didn't say it aloud; he could barely talk. But he bobbed his head. Prestle, Jackson moved his head up and down when I asked him to leave it to me.

"Then Pearl materialized unannounced with her kids and took the ranch away from me. I had already made several plans. And I will include you in my plans, my dear. I stand to make millions if I, I mean, we, can get my hands on that land." Glorieta gulped the whisky and, with a wicked glint in her eyes, said, "I know what I have to do."

"I'm sure you do, Glo. Now, show me that beautiful lacy bra you promised."

"I bought this with you in mind," she seductively murmured in his ears. Unbuttoning her blouse, Glorieta sensuously danced the cha-cha-cha in front of Prestle. With his head buried in her voluptuous bosom, she glanced furtively at her wristwatch. When he gasped for air, she teasingly muttered, "Remember last time? Your blood pressure and such? You need to take it easy from now on. Okay?" Glorieta hastily buttoned her blouse and then dashed for her car in the bank's parking lot.

The Slippery Scheme

Glorieta pulled in front of Pearl's catering office. During the last few days, she had frequently gone there at the end of the day to say hello to Pearl and to place future orders for the bank. She tried the door. It was unlocked. She knew perfectly that at this time of the day, the kitchen floor would be covered with soapy water, very slippery, like an ice-skating rink. Pearl was in her office, unaware of Glorieta's presence. Pearl's helper, Lourdes, was refilling the bucket with fresh water at the outdoor sink in the backyard.

Perfect! Glorieta deviously smiled. She quickly messed up her hair, making it resemble a short, spiked lion's mane. Then, she lowered herself to the soapy floor and screamed, her voice echoing throughout the room. Pearl stormed out of her office and saw Glorieta on the wet floor, groaning. She quickly bent over and tried to calm Glorieta down. Lourdes approached apologetically.

"I can't get up." Glorieta grimaced as she tried to stand up. "I think something's broken." She pretended that she couldn't get up on her own.

Lourdes wanted to lift her, but Pearl put out an arm to stop her. "Let's call an ambulance."

"No, no," Glorieta objected. She managed to put herself into a sitting position, wincing dramatically. "I don't want to cause a fuss. I'm going to be okay."

Pearl asked Lourdes to put dry towels on the floor, get an ice pack, and pull up a chair. Pearl helped the moaning Glorieta move up into the chair. Pearl couldn't afford a lawsuit. She'd lose everything.

"The ice pack and a glass of water will be enough," Glorieta insisted.

A sudden movement by the front window caught the corner of her vision. She glanced up to see a pair of eyes protected by the brim of a baseball cap eyeing the scene. The person disappeared before Glorieta could figure out who it was.

Aided by the two women, Glorieta limped slowly to her car. Then, the women waved goodbyes. Glorieta drove away and asked her image in the mirror, "Did someone see me fake that fall? I hope I didn't ruin my Prada suit for nothing!"

***

"A promotion will lead me to my own place. Marriage is not a bad idea," Johnny convinced himself while looking at the rearview mirror of his VW Beetle. He was driving slowly and approaching the house of the girl with the revealing top.

In that quiet neighborhood, cars didn't pass by very often. But when the girl heard the sound of the car near her house, she quickly walked towards her iron gate and stood on the sidewalk. When Johnny drove by, she bent her body sensually and touched her toned and sun-kissed calf. In that position, she locked eyes with Johnny, who raised his eyebrows subtly.

Johnny could still see her image in his side door mirror as he pulled at Fabiana's house. She and Manuelito were just getting off the bike.

"Evenin'. How's it going, honey Bee?" Johnny greeted Fabiana with his usual endearment as soon as he stepped out of the car. He hugged her tightly and kissed her lightly on her lips. Fabiana glanced toward the ruined suit jacket on the passenger seat.

"Oh, don't worry about the suit. I'm getting a new one soon for a special occasion. Boy, am I tired! I had an extremely hectic day. Is your mom in?"

"Pardon?"

"I have something I need to ask her."

"I'll get her," Manuelito said.

A few minutes later, Pearl entered the living room, followed by Manuelito and casually greeted, "Hi, Johnny. Sit down."

Johnny walked to the couch but changed his mind and said, "Pearl, I sat all day at work today." Fanning himself and passing his hand on his shining and sweaty forehead, Johnny stood by the front door.

"What's the matter?" Fabiana asked him.

"Bee, you know I'm not one for yada-yada talking. If your father were here, I'd talk to him. So, I'll talk to your mom." He cleaned his throat and looked uncomfortable. "Pearl, the thing is, I'm here to make it official and ask your permission to marry your daughter."

"Johnny!" Fabiana loudly shrieked in surprise.

"Wait a minute. Manuelito, darling, go do your homework. Dinner will be ready in half an hour."

"Okay." Manuelito had once told his mom he wasn't in agreement with selling the ranch ever. But today, teasing his sister, he looked at her and, walking like a bride and humming the wedding march, went to his bedroom.

"Now, where were we?" Pearl was relieved Johnny hadn't come to demand compensation for Glorieta's accident. Pearl wondered if Johnny even knew about it.

"Pearl, I've been working for the bank for almost three years already, so I have a good job," Johnny proudly said. "That's when it dawned on me. It's time for me to settle down and be a family man. I think… I think your daughter will make me very happy."

"What about making her very happy, Johnny?" Pearl countered calmly.

"I promise to make her the happiest woman in the world."

"Can you give the world to my daughter?" Pearl continued.

Before Johnny had the chance to reply, there was an urgent knock at the door. He glanced through the peephole, zooming in on a woman's low-cut, sweetheart neckline. "Two women," he whispered. Johnny recognized that one of them was the seductive girl he'd seen by the iron gate.

The Attraction

Johnny finally opened the door to let the women in. Carole fluffed her hair and pretended not to notice him. Ula spoke in an urgent voice. "Pearl, don't you watch soap operas? We are desperate to know what's going to happen tonight. My son locked himself in his room with the TV."

"Didn't you say Nico is claustrophobic?" asked Fabiana.

"Yes, if the door is locked from the outside. Not if he locks the door. He's still mad at us, so he put the TV in his room," Ula explained.

Fabiana turned the TV on. Pearl got up and asked Fabiana to help her in the kitchen.

"Darling, you and Johnny are such a lovely couple."

Fabiana rolled her eyes and returned to the living room. She caught Johnny seated next to Carole, furtively looking at Carole's cleavage. Noticing Johnny's gaze on her chest, Carole took a deep breath, sat up straight, and tightened her midriff. Johnny fidgeted, opening and closing his hands. Ula was seated in the armchair with her face almost touching the TV screen.

The opening scene of "The Prospect of Change" showed a Baccarat Vase. The title and credits were rolling to the sound of a melancholic song. Ula said she loved the lyrics. Carole brought her index finger to her lips. "Mom, don't sing, please."

The stars came into view. Ula explained the backstory of the show, "Stewart has to be there. They are auctioning Rose Crown's items. She was a TV pioneer. He wants a piece of history."

Only Johnny acknowledged Ula. He nodded and smiled.

Ula interrupted several times during the hour-long episode: "I'm sure he will want some of her journals… No way! He wants the vase!?! I can't believe it!" Carole, Johnny, and Fabiana kept their gaze on the TV and ignored her as best they could.

During the commercial break, Pearl came in from the kitchen and offered refreshments.

"Whatever you are cooking smells good," Johnny said.

"It's chicken wings. Does anybody want some?"

"My favorite," Carole said and licked her lips mischievously in Johnny's direction, causing his legs to fidget convulsively.

Haunting music from the soap opera filled the air. "Hey, the show is back on," Ula said. She continued her monologue as if the actors could hear her. "No, Megan, you can't take anything... Mark my words, Megan, Rose's granddaughter, will want to keep everything...Watch this. The UPS man will say he slept with Rose. He thinks she is Rose Brown. But she is Rose Crown. I know because I read it in the magazine." Ula and Carole laughed out loud, startling both Johnny and Fabiana. "See? Wasn't that funny?" Ula said, "I think Cindy wants to keep the Baccarat vase. The daughter wants silk roses."

Johnny was the only one who looked at Ula. He nodded.

At the next commercial break, Ula got up. Manuelito entered the room and distributed utensils and paper products. Pearl brought the platter of chicken wings in lemon and mustard sauce and asked them to help themselves. Being the last one to serve herself, Carole kept the tray on her lap. Johnny and Ula wanted seconds. Carole got confused as to whom to pass the platter first and moved it sideways, splashing sauce on Johnny's trousers.

Johnny looked at the stain and at Carole and said with a forgiving tone of voice, "Oh! No problem."

Fabiana frowned, thinking that just a few hours ago, Johnny had been furious about the stain on his jacket caused by her painting.

Ula laughed. "This happens to us all the time. My daughter and I play this back-and-forth tray game." Dismissing the stain as if it were nothing, she said, "It's just sauce. I'm sure you have a good dry cleaner."

The show was back. Carole hushed her mother, encouraging her to watch TV.

Megan shouted, "One thousand." There was a whisper around the auction room. "One thousand dollars, going once, going twice..." The camera zoomed in on Cindy, who was nodding and smiling approvingly. And to the mother and daughter's delight and patrons' disbelief, Cindy and Megan ended up bidding and bringing home the majority of "Rose's memories" listed in the catalog.

"I'm happy that Cindy kept her mother's stuff," said Ula.

"Me, too," Carole agreed, her breathing making her upper torso move up and down rhythmically. Johnny was hypnotized by Carole's cotton eyelet blouse.

Carole and Ula got up and left, saying the food was delicious. Johnny stood up and held his paper plate in front of his stained trousers and was about to follow the two women when Pearl stopped him.

"So?"

"Pardon?" asked Johnny.

"Are you able to show the world to Fabiana?"

"Oh, sure!" Johnny smiled and said, "We can marry. And you won't need to work, honey Bee. I'll get promoted work for both of us. I'm sure you'll be busy raising our family."

"Mom. I can't think about marriage right now. Sorry."

"No problem," Johnny muttered and rushed to his car. He slowly drove by Carole's house. Closing the iron gate, Carole kept her gaze on Johnny.

"What's her name?" He realized nobody ever addressed the girl by her name.

***

Later in the night, Johnny couldn't shake the thought of the girl's name. "I've got to find out her name," Johnny said out loud during his shower. Under the hot stream of water, Johnny suddenly felt dizzy and weak. He lowered the temperature, and the cold water restored a little bit of his energy. He went to the kitchen. Ceeda was not home but cooked another batch of mashed potatoes for dinner. He gave a big sigh, got a bowl, and helped himself with a generous portion of the creamy potatoes. The memory of Carole licking her lips replayed vividly in his mind, an image that seemed to linger longer than he anticipated. The subtle gesture, a mix of allure and anticipation, was etched in his thoughts, leaving an impression that played on a loop, stirring a range of emotions within him.

A New Tour Gig

Fabiana was drinking coffee on the porch and telling Pearl, who was tending to her containers of seeds and sweet potatoes slips, that she had sent her curriculum vitae to the resorts nearby. The phone rang, and Manuelito answered it. "Fabiana, for you."

"Speaking," Fabiana said and listened. "Who?"... "Yes. I can be there in an hour." She relayed to her mother that she had just accepted an on-call tour guide position. A few minutes later, she hailed a cab to the resort office near Jungle City.

A familiar voice startled her. "Hello again. I came across your curriculum. Glad you are back in town and could come in on such short notice. I'll drive; you do the talking." Fabiana was speechless. Paolo was in front of her. She did not know what to say. It seemed as if her tongue was paralyzed as she just gazed at Paolo.

Paolo seemed unhinged. Before the awkwardness could make either of them uncomfortable, he continued what he was saying. "We'll be picking up our guests, two couples and their children, at the resort." He gave her a printout saying, "I'm sure you're familiar with the birds, but please take a few minutes to read the narration of the tour."

Paolo drove about three miles south on a road punctuated by curves and bumps. From the front seat, Fabiana swiveled to inspect a cooler in the car's back seat. The ice was melting fast. She asked Paolo to make a stop at a convenience store. While she was in the store, Paulo was busy revising the guest list. Unexpectedly, a truck driver rear-ended Paolo's car and drove off while cursing at Paolo. The unexpected impact threw Paolo forward.

Fabiana hurried to the driver's side of the car and asked, "Are you okay?"

"My shoulder," complained Paolo.

"Here, apply some of these ice cubes. Do you need to go to the hospital?"

"No. One of the guests is a doctor. Perhaps he can help me."

"You rest, I'll drive."

"Okay. This is the second time in a week that I've hurt my shoulder." Paolo said.

"How so?"

"A few days ago, I tripped and fell into a hole in the ground, which was covered with plants, and landed on my right side. I wasn't strong enough to pull myself up. My right arm was useless, so I had to brace my left elbow on a root and get my feet under me. Then, I used a big tree branch as a staff to return to the resort. I thought I was okay after that, but now my right shoulder really hurts."

Fabiana was captivated by listening to the sound of Paolo's voice.

Their guests, wearing hats with neck flaps, waited at the entrance of the resort.

"Hello, everybody. Sorry for the delay. I'm Paolo, the boat driver, and this is Fabiana, the bird expert. We had an incident on the way over and were hoping Dr. Leeland could quickly assess my shoulder. If it's not too much trouble."

"Of course," the doctor replied, examining Paolo's shoulders. "Paolo, it's slightly out of place. I'll put it back into its proper position. Let's head up to my room."

In the doctor's room, his wife handed him a muscle-relaxing cream.

Fabiana helped Paolo remove his Polo shirt, and the doctor applied the cream, advising, "Re-apply this cream every three hours."

Fabiana found it impossible to avert her gaze from Paolo's bare and muscular torso while Paolo gazed back at her. There was an unspoken tension in the air as Paolo sat on the bed half-naked. The tension, however, did not last long as the doctor popped the shoulder back into place.

"Thank you, Dr. Leeland. I'm fine now. Ready for your tour?" Paolo asked, rotating his shoulders. He wanted to pay, but the doctor refused payment, so Paolo said his tour was on the house. "I'm going to take care of it."

Paolo was the first to enter the long boat. Extending his good arm, he helped all of the guests inside the boat.

Fabiana was concerned that the boat seemed very unstable. She whispered in Paolo's ears, "Are there piranhas in the water?"

He nodded, turned to the tourists and said, "Please don't put your hands in water. This river contains piranhas."

Fabiana reviewed the remaining safety precautions with the guests who were fastening their life vests.

During the river tour, Paolo and Fabiana answered the guests' questions. "Yes, there are jaguars in this area. They are the largest feline in the Americas."... "Jaguars are nocturnal hunters."..."Yes, jaguars take a nap during the day across the branch of a tree they mark as their own. The shade of the trees offers jaguars protection from the heat... They hunt caimans, capybaras, and other animals."

Fabiana also pointed to capybaras, giant anteaters, caimans, monkeys, large nests, and colorful birds. The guests adjusted their binoculars and were excited when locating the animals and birds. "See those large nests? They are made by jabirus birds about the size of an American flamingo."

"What are those?" One of the guests asked, pointing to a tree.

"That is called a Pink Trumpet Tree," Fabiana answered. "The flowers with slight ruffled petals are pretty amazing, big, like trumpet shapes. They can also be referred as Tabebuia rosea."

"Are these poisonous?"

"There is information indicating that Tabebuia trees are toxic or poisonous. In general, the trees are cultivated for their ornamental value and the beauty of their flowers."

"Oh, okay. Thanks!" The guest said.

Upon returning to the resort, Fabiana and Paolo thanked the guests and walked around the courtyard. "You left Rio for good?" Paolo asked.

"Back to my roots, yes. What about you?"

Tiny frogs jumped in front of the doorways facing the courtyard. The frogs made a loud sound that ricocheted off the walls. *I don't need to kiss a frog*, Fabiana thought. *My prince may be right here beside me.* Fabiana had never felt so strongly for anyone before. It felt as if her heartbeat got faster with every second she spent with Paolo. All she wanted to do was gaze at Paolo's face.

Paolo waved his good arm at one of the frogs to scare it away, and the frog hopped into the bush. "It depends. I'm working on my family tree. I'm following the trail of one of my more adventurous ancestors. I followed him to Rio, but he'd already left. Then, I heard he was in central Brazil. So, I accepted this job in the Pantanal."

Paolo wrote the word P. IVA on a piece of paper and gave it to Fabiana. If you come across this name, please let me know." Gazing into Paolo's greenish amber eyes, she envisioned them morphing into the eyes of a jaguar. Desire, mutually reflecting in Paolo's eyes, led her to playfully ponder, *Who's the jaguar? - Who's the prey?*

They parted ways with big smiles on their faces. After meeting Paolo, Fabiana was happy and feeling on top of the world.

She was enthralled by the sunset and the graceful return of flocks of birds to their trees in the Pantanal. She tried to paint the shades of orange, pink, and purple that reflected off the calm waters.

Fabiana started waking up early to witness the sunrise, not only to observe the transition from darkness to light but to enjoy a moment of serenity, beauty, and the promise of a new day in the heart of nature.

***

After leaving Pearl's office, Glorieta stopped at the Jungle City Beauty Salon, got rid of the soapy foam in her hair, and got a facial and a back massage. She returned home with a growling stomach.

In the kitchen, she opened the lid of the single pan on the stove and smirked. Holding the pan in one hand and its lid in the other, she went to Johnny's bedroom. Pushing his bedroom door open, she stood by the door frame and, for a few seconds, watched her son as he slumbered restlessly. Vengefully, she crashed the metallic lid against the empty pan as if they were cymbals.

Startled, Johnny stared at her, groaned, and ignored her.

"Johnny, do you think Ceeda cooks for you only? You will have a bellyache, you glutton." Shutting his bedroom door, she returned to the kitchen, where she got a bottle of red wine and the tallest wine glass from the cabinet. With tight lips, she marched to her bedroom and put the wine and glass on the night table. She kicked her high heels off her feet, turned on the TV, propped herself in bed and then poured wine to the brim of the glass and drank half of it as if it was water.

After a few minutes of watching the soap opera, she turned the TV off. "I should be on TV, not these second-rate actresses," Glorieta said. "Nobody does a convincing dizzy spell like me. My performance today at Pearl's was really suitable for an Oscar."

Changing her voice, she replayed her fake fall in her mind. "Oh, Pearl, my head is spinning like that ceiling fan. Please turn it off, dear." She poured more wine and chuckled. "Lourdes tiptoeing on the soapy floor covered with towels to turn the fan off...Lourdes and Pearl helped me like two crutches towards my car. Priceless."

Glorieta impersonated Lourdes, "Dear Lord, forgive me, I didn't know Glorieta would be in the office..." and mocked Pearl, "Are you sure you can drive... I'm so sorry. Keep me posted, okay?"

112

Chugging the remaining wine, Glorieta slurred, "You betcha I will. I'll sue you. Rancho Santa Fabiana will be mine. Wait and see, bitch!"

Suddenly, Glorieta frowned, "Was someone there by the window when I lay on the floor?" She smoothed her forehead. "Nah, it was just a bird, I'm sure. Stupid birds."

***

Manuelito rode his bike to his mom's catering business to pick up the orders for delivery. Unbeknownst to him, from inside a phone booth on the other side of the street, a man watched. His phone call was brief, "I see the boy. Let me know what's next." He nodded, hung up the phone and walked away.

Pearl got a tray of hot cupcakes and markers with the words *banana nut, strawberry, and chocolate chip* on one side and the image of a jaguar on the other. "Look at these cute jaguar markers that your sister just created for me. I need to identify each cupcake, then off you go."

"Wait a minute, Mom. I'm hungry. Where's my Caprese sandwich?"

The Girl's Name

It was past 6 PM when Johnny parked in front of Fabiana's house. He got out of the car and stood on the sidewalk. His eyes surveyed the area to the south, hoping to see the girl with the revealing top. No luck tonight. He turned his attention to the vast piece of land to the north.

It was that time of the day when birds returned. All sorts of birds were returning to their tree nests. He looked up and was blinded by the sun shining brightly on its way to sunset. He closed his eyes and took cover under a tree as a flock of colorful birds flew low in the sky. Their sheer quantity scared him. He threw up his arms to protect his head from bird droppings. They'd hit him before. It could happen again.

Fabiana rushed outside the kitchen door to watch the flock of birds flying over her house.

Johnny knocked on the front door and waited for a response. His face was bathed in sweat from the oppressive humidity. He removed his tie and put it in the pocket of his jacket. He knocked again, this time harder.

When Manuelito opened the door, Johnny was rubbing his face as if he had an invisible towel. Drying his sweaty hand on his pants, Johnny offered a handshake. Suppressing his disgust, Manuelito closed his hand and greeted him with a fist bump instead.

"Is Fabiana in?"

As Johnny was entering the room, Manuelito said, "Oh, hello there." Carole and Ula entered right behind Johnny and asked Manuelito to turn the TV on. Ula said the soap opera was about to start, and their TV was still locked in her son's bedroom.

"The armchair is mine, Carole," Ula said. "You'll get your own chair when you have your own home or get married." She turned to Johnny and said, "She's twenty, still living at home."

So her name is Carole! Johnny thought. Discreetly eyeing Carole, who was fixing her revealing top, Johnny confided to Ula, "I'll leave my mother's house only when I get married."

Ula nodded and turned her attention to the TV screen.

Johnny bragged, "I can afford to live independently, but there aren't many places to rent or buy."

While Johnny looked around the room, Ula and Carole exchanged a whispered message. "He's a great catch." Ula mouthed.

"I know. Working on it." Carole mouthed back.

Johnny turned to Carole, "Besides, I like to eat…." Johnny and Carole locked eyes for an instant."… the food prepared by Ceeda."

"Ceeda?" Carole asked with curiosity in her eyes.

"Yes, the maid, she's the best cook…"

Pearl came home from work and was not surprised to see Johnny, Carole, and Ula in her living room watching the soap opera. Overhearing the reference to Ceeda, she teased, "Is that right, Johnny?"

"Pearl. Nice to see you. What I mean is that there's room in my heart for cooks. You are my second favorite cook in the whole world."

Outside in the backyard, Fabiana was amazed by the sight of the stork-like birds with their white body plumage, black necks, and long black bills returning to their trees in the jungle. She dreamed of working with Paolo again, sharing nature's bountiful supply of exotic and colorful birds with him and their clients.

Fabiana entered the living room and was surprised by Johnny's presence. She wished he'd call before coming over.

Johnny apologized.

Fabiana couldn't stop herself from comparing Johnny's groveling behavior with Paolo's self-confidence. The wild gaze in Paolo's intense amber eyes always reminded her of the eyes of the jaguar.

Johnny squeezed between Carole and Fabiana to watch the soap opera. As usual, Ula spoke over the actors, explaining what was happening on the show. Pearl made corned beef sandwiches for their guests.

Ula asked, "How about soft drinks, like *Guarana*?"

Fabiana looked at her mother and said, "I'm sorry. We have no soft drink."

Ula took a bite of her sandwich and, with her eyes glued on the TV screen, said, "Water is fine, then."

Carole inserted her hands under her leg, pushing her breasts forward.

Johnny fidgeted and lowered his hands to the side of his legs. He felt the warmth of Carole's hand as she inconspicuously slid a piece of paper under his hand. Johnny's eyes widened in surprise. "Wa, water for me too, please."

Johnny excused himself, went to the bathroom, and read Carole's note. He returned to the living room with a concerned gaze on his face and said something had come up, and he needed to leave. Bending to kiss Fabiana goodbye, he inadvertently stepped on Carole's foot.

Carole winced, and her mouth fell open for a very brief moment.

Fabiana tilted her head to avoid Johnny's kiss, and her nose bumped into his. She massaged her nose, smiled, said she would call him, and with a slight shudder, returned her attention to the TV.

Johnny mumbled that he was sorry, straightened and started winking as if he had something in his eyes.

Carole took Johnny's wink as a sign.

Sweet Encounters and Hidden Desires

Johnny drove to the ice cream parlor on Main Street and, during the short ride, kept rolling his neck and shoulders. After parking, he climbed out of the car and searched the sidewalk. A few minutes later, he beamed at the goddess undulating towards him.

"I read your note," he said. "Ice cream?" He raised his eyebrow seductively.

"Two scoops, chocolate, and peanut butter," Carole said firmly.

"No way, you like peanuts?"

The server handed Carole her cone.

"My favorite," Carole said.

"So, I have competition."

"Maybe," Carole teased, licking the soft ice cream slowly.

The cashier was slower than usual. Johnny asked Carole to hold his cone while he paid. Due to the heat, the ice cream melted onto her hands in seconds.

They sat at a table under the canopy of a mango tree. Johnny's eyes drifted from Carole's red fingernails to her red lips moistened by the melting ice cream.

"So, Johnny, are you dating?" Carole broke the spell.

"It's complicated."

"I'm not a jealous type, you know. Be happy... fulfill your dreams. What is your dream?"

My dream? I thought it was Fabiana. But now I want to defy my mother. And she wants me to marry Fabiana. "I'd be more interested in your dreams, beautiful lady. Do you have a dream?"

"I dream of enjoying this ice cream. Having my own TV... wearing what I want... going fishing."

A print of *The Birth of Venus*, by Botticelli, that Johnny had on the wall of his bedroom flashed into his mind. Carole looked like Venus emerging from the sea, and her revealing eyelet top resembled a fishing net encircling her curvy nude body.

"I like fishing," Johnny said, taking her sticky hand into his. "We should go fishing someday." They laughed and rubbed their sticky hands together.

Nico passed by without seeing them.

"There goes my brother," Carol said. "Sorry Johnny, if I don't catch him, we'll never get our TV back. It's locked in his bedroom." She kissed his cheeks before dashing down the street and calling Nico's name.

The sensation of the kiss on the corner of his lips stayed with Johnny all the way home.

***

Glorieta left the house early. A lawsuit based on her fake fall at Pearl's catering business would not go very far. Her best bet to win Rancho Santa Fabiana was to involve Fabiana's brother, Manuelito.

Johnny woke up with excessive sweating and intense bone pain. He brought his hand to his nose and then stared at the blood on his hand. He rushed to the bathroom, put toilet paper in each nostril, tilted his head backward, and to alleviate the pain, he fell to his knees and bent forward. A few minutes later, he called Ceeda.

The cook hurried to the bathroom door.

Johnny moaned.

Ceeda knocked. "What's the matter?" She knocked again. "Johnny."

Johnny got up slowly and steadied himself on the sink basin, feeling dizzy and barely able to breathe the nauseating fumes emanating from the toilet. He splashed water on his sweaty face while blood continued to drip from his nose to the white sink. He looked at his image in the mirror. Unshaved and with disheveled hair, he looked fatigued. Ceeda knocked again.

Noticeably distressed, Johnny opened the door and threw his two-hundred-pound frame at Ceeda, who, at her age, wasn't able to hold more than two little kittens in her thin arms.

Ceeda took a few steps backward and steadied herself on her back on the corridor wall while Johnny slumped against her. She managed to squirm out from under Johnny's weight and lowered him down on the floor with his face to the side. She shoved a towel under his bleeding nose. Johnny asked her to call for help before he crawled to his bedroom.

Ceeda didn't know Glorieta's whereabouts, but she found a number for Joao Paiva, Johnny's father, in the Rolodex.

Love, Loss, and Redemption in the Jungle

Johnny's father's name was, in reality, John P. Iva, but locals changed this to Joao Paiva when he moved here. He didn't seem to mind this nickname and even adopted it for himself.

In 1955, upon receiving his bachelor's degree in forest biology from Virginia Tech College, Joao accepted a paid internship as an arborist in Rio de Janeiro, which led to a full-time position at the Brazilian Pantanal. He fell in love with the Pantanal's rich tropical flora and decided to make it his home. In 1960, he met and married Glorieta. But their marriage ended the day after Johnny's tenth birthday.

That was in 1972. That day, out of the blue, Johnny's nose wouldn't stop bleeding. Glorieta blamed the nosebleed on Johnny's selfishness for not sharing his candy with her. She asked Joao to take care of the boy because she had an appointment for a haircut. Joao took Johnny to the emergency room. Assured that his son was stable and would be released in the afternoon, Joao returned to his office.

But fires started by a group of greedy investors ravaged Joao's office and destroyed the farms around it and a large section of the jungle. Suffering from smoke inhalation and a critical burn encircling his left hand, Joao was taken to a hospital in another part of the state, where he stayed for a couple of months.

Glorieta never forgave Joao for abandoning little Johnny in Jungle City Hospital. She immediately served Joao with divorce papers and won full custody of Johnny.

Joao devoted the intervening years to saving the jungle's ecosystem.

The phone rang in Joao's house.

Ceeda pleaded, "Answer, please, come on." She was about to hang up the phone when a voice on the other side said hello.

Joao dried the sweat from his leathered and wrinkled forehead and listened to Ceeda's account of Johnny's collapse. "I'm coming over," he said.

Joao parked his car a block away and hurried to Johnny's house. Ceeda was at the front door waiting for him and took him to Johnny's bedroom.

Joao knelt beside his ailing son, who was moaning in pain on the floor. Taking his temperature, Joao made the decision to take him to the hospital in Jungle City. Joao had only one thought on the way to the hospital: *I will never abandon you, son.*

***

Glorieta didn't come home for lunch. Ceeda picked up the phone directory, opened it to the page listing beauty parlors, and started calling and asking to speak with Glorieta. She got lucky on her second attempt.

Glorieta told the young receptionist she'd return the call later.

Ceeda insisted on speaking to her immediately.

Glorieta marched into the reception area and barked into the phone, "What is the problem, *criatura*?" No one in the beauty parlor paid attention to Glorieta, but she looked around the room with a phony smile on her face. The smile suddenly changed into a concerned expression. Glorieta ordered the beautician to remove the cream on her face. "An unforeseen situation at home requires my attention. Bill me later," she said and left.

Emergency Response

Glorieta's high heels thumped noisily on the kitchen floor.

Ceeda sat at the table praying, "Dear Lord, help Johnny."

"Ceeda. Why on earth did you call Joao?" Glorieta sniffed the air and fanned herself, "Pee-ew. Clean Johnny's bathroom with a full bottle of PineSol when I leave. Now, tell me, *criatura*..." After listening to Ceeda, Glorieta said, "Ok. Stop your crying. I'm going to the hospital."

Hiding his eyes behind the brim of his baseball cap, Nico, Carole's brother, trailed Glorieta as she marched from her house toward her car parked a few blocks away. As she was unlocking the door, he stepped around her and, without warning, closed the door, trapping Glorieta between him and the vehicle.

"Don't even think about screaming," he said, his lips touching her ear.

A pungent odor coming from Nico's mouth reminded Glorieta of Johnny's stinky bathroom. She wished she had PineSol cleaning product to throw at her assailant's face. She was frightened but managed to demand, "Take my car if you want. Let go of me."

"Car?" Nico threatened, "I know what you did at Pearl's business yesterday."

The attacker pinned Glorieta against the door, her stomach pressed hard against it. She moved her head and caught a glimpse of the guy's baseball cap and realized he might be the same person who was peeking inside Pearl's catering business the day before. "I don't know what you are saying," she said.

"I can keep it just between you and me," he said, pressing on her arms.

"Get off me. If my housekeeper sees you here, she'll call the police." Glorieta cursed the faceless drivers that kept parking in front of her own house, forcing her to park blocks away where Ceeda would never be able to see this assault.

He turned her face to him. His mouth was barely two inches from her nose. "If anyone sees us, they'll think we are kissing. Now, back to my proposal."

Disgusted, she turned her face to avoid his bad breath.

"Pearl…"

"I'm not Pearl."

"I know," he said. "I'm simply saying the name Pearl to jog your memory," he said. "You know, from yesterday… when you were throwing yourself on the soapy floor? Ring a bell?"

Glorieta let out a sigh of relief, "You seem like such a nice young man. Can I get some breathing room? Let's talk like the good people that we are." She pushed him away gently and faced him. "Hey, I recognize you. Are you in financial trouble? Is that why you are here?" Glorieta asked with an agenda in mind.

"Yes! An esteemed member of our society like yourself could do wonders to help me."

"Oh, young fella, you have the wrong idea of me."

He closed his fist, hit the car door and grabbed her wrists in each of his hands. "I want a partnership."

Glorieta tried not to show any fear. "A partnership? That's intriguing. Why didn't you say so right away? Would you be willing to run a few errands?"

"It depends on the pay."

"Look. I'm in a hurry right now. Is there a place we can meet later tonight? I do have something that will interest you."

"Fine, but don't play games with me. I know where you live."

"Sure. What's your name?"

"For now, call me partner. I'll tell you my name if all goes well tonight." In the blink of an eye, he sprinted around the block and disappeared from Glorieta's view.

Glorieta took in a big breath. Relieved but shaken, she smelled the collar of her jacket. "That creep ruined my brand new Prada. It stinks like a sewer." She removed the jacket, threw it on the back seat, and sped away to the hospital.

***

The doctor asked Johnny a few questions, checked Johnny's vitals and blood pressure, palpated his abdomen, and ordered a battery of tests.

Glorieta arrived at the hospital and spoke with paramedics rolling a gurney to the emergency room. She was directed to the receptionist, who raised her hand to request a moment to finish her phone conversation. Glorieta tapped her foot, drummed her fingers on the counter, and scornfully checked out the people occupying the seats in the waiting area.

She squinted her eyes and pursed her lips. One of them was Joao, her ex-husband. They had been separated for over a decade. She marched over to him. "I know what you've been up to, you jerk. Your little school teacher girlfriend is pathetic and a gold digger. How dare you?"

Joao didn't respond. He was used to Glorieta's irrational eruptions. No doubt the jungle's pseudo socialites, who only cared about gossip and the latest brand name in accessories, had slipped this juicy tidbit into Glorieta's ear simply to enjoy her explosion.

"You better not be giving that gold digger any of my money, or you'll be hearing from my attorney."

"Lower your voice. Now is hardly the time to discuss finances. Aren't you interested in how our son is doing?"

"That's what I'm here for. What happened?" A few minutes later, she shouted, "All this commotion over a nosebleed?"

People around them began to take notice. Embarrassed, Joao sank into his chair without another word.

Glorieta stomped back over to the receptionist, got her visitor's pass, and went to Johnny's room. She found him asleep, so she left, shaking her head in disgust.

The doctor called Joao into a private consultation room, where he disclosed his findings. Joao left the doctor's office in shock. "The leukemia has returned. The chemo didn't work. Only a bone

124

marrow transplant can save him now. Lord help us." At the hospital lab, Joao rolled up his sleeve for a blood draw, hoping to be a match.

A Rush Catering Drop-Off

Manuelito parked the bike in the backyard of his house, entered the kitchen and asked, "Is dinner ready, Mom? I'm so hungry...These cupcakes look delicious…"

Pearl was placing markers designed by Fabiana in the cupcakes and said, "Sorry, Manuelito, these are a rush order. The customer specifically asked for it to be delivered at six o'clock. How about a slice of the freshly baked *kibbeh*?" Pearl served her children.

"That was really good, Mom," Fabiana said.

"I'm still hungry. I want more," Manuelito brought his plate forward while gulping the last spoonful.

"I'm happy you both like it. Just because we live in the jungle, we don't have to forget our good manners, right? May I? And chew food first, remember?"

Manuelito lightly shrugged his shoulder, moved his empty dish up and down in front of his mother, and teased, "You are a wonderful cook, Mom. May I have some more?"

"Sure, help yourself."

Pearl glanced at her watch and handed Manuelito the Tupperware container of cupcakes. "Here's the address, son. Bring the container back, please. Off you go."

Manuelito returned in less than an hour, placing the full container of cupcakes on the dining table. "The client canceled and refused to pay, so I brought them back."

"That's the third canceled order in a row." Pearl sat down, feeling the weight of the world on her shoulders. "What's going on?"

"I'm sorry, Mom," Fabiana said. "Who ordered them?"

"Glorieta, on behalf of her friends. You kids might as well eat them."

"Glorieta should pay for these. I'll call her this minute." Fabiana went into the living room to dial Johnny's home number.

There was a light tapping on the door, which Fabiana, Pearl and Manuelito ignored.

The door opened from the outside. "Pearl," Ula entered, gasping for air, followed by Carole, "Nico locked our TV in his room again. We can't miss tonight's episode. My cousin, Veronica Luz, will appear as a doctor." Ula inhaled and said, "Wow, something smells wonderful. It must be Pearl's famous cupcakes." She moistened her lips at the sight of the freshly baked cupcakes on the dining table.

Ceeda answered Fabiana's call on the first ring. Fabiana asked for Glorieta, but Ceeda rushed to tell her all about Johnny.

"Ceeda, please slow down. Jungle City Hospital? What are the visitor's hours?"

Staring blankly at the TV, Carole eavesdropped on Fabiana's conversation.

"I'll visit Johnny first thing tomorrow morning," Fabiana said. "I'm so sorry."

Carole whispered to Ula, "Poor Johnny. He and Fabiana can't be an item. Just look at her reaction. I'd have gone to the hospital immediately."

Manuelito was about to get a cupcake when Ula begged that he turn on the TV first. He obliged, then got a cupcake and went to the backyard, where he got his bike and rode towards Main Street.

Fabiana slowly put the phone back on the cradle. "Mom, Johnny got a nosebleed and fainted. He's at Jungle City Hospital."

They heard a knock, and after peeking through the peephole, Pearl opened the door to a sweaty young man in his twenties. She arched her eyebrows when he explained that he was there to collect past-due grocery bills.

"How much do I owe you?" Pearl asked.

"Two hundred and fifty." Fanning himself, the bill collector asked for a glass of water.

Pearl went to the kitchen and returned with a glass of water. Then she went to her bedroom to get her wallet. Carole jumped up from the couch and followed her.

"Pearly," she said charmingly. "Do you have a minute? I owe that guy as well. Could you help me?"

"Carole, I need you to pay me back. Did you get the medicine for your brother?"

"Yes. But Nico's still not well. I need another one hundred. If you don't have it, I don't know what I'm going to do," Carole muttered. "I promise to pay back everything this weekend. Hopefully, I'll sell more Tupperware. Who knows."

With serious misgivings, Pearl counted out five twenties and handed them to Carole. They returned to the living room. Pearl paid the man what she owed, and he requested another glass of water.

The bill collector stuck his head inside. "My lucky day. Carole's here. I need a few Tupperware products."

"Peppy?" Carole said. "Is that you? Goodness, heavens, man! Serendipity. I was thinking about you. Let's go to my house. You can select what you want from my stock." Carole turned to Ula and said she would be right back.

Keeping her eyes glued to the TV, Ula mumbled, "My daughter was born to be in sales."

Fabiana joined her mother at the door, and both women watched Carole and the collector stroll down the street with their arms intertwined.

Carole returned an hour later, after the show had ended, boasting her debts were cleared, and that the man had even bought Tupperware products worth two hundred and ninety seven dollars.

Pearl immediately asked for her money back, but Ula interrupted.

"Carole, I have to fill you in on everything you missed." Ula unwrapped a cupcake and took a big bite. "Cousin Roni is such a great actress. She called Champ, her ex-boyfriend of years past and urged him to come to the hospital to visit her son Ollion, who is very ill. What's going to happen next? Only cousin Roni knows. I shall call her."

Fabiana glanced at the time on her watch – eleven o'clock. She stretched her arms and suppressed a yawn before announcing her intention to retire for the night.

Ula stood up and eyed the three cupcakes left on the table. When Pearl suggested she take them home, Ula didn't hesitate. She waved goodbye with the container of cupcakes in her hands.

Pearl said goodnight to Manuelito through his closed bedroom door, unaware that he had not yet come home.

***

Glorieta returned home from the hospital and was annoyed to find all the parking places in front of her house were taken. Then Nico appeared and motioned for her to park a half block away. With an irritated thump on the dashboard, she followed his suggestion, parked where he indicated, and stepped out of the vehicle.

"So, did you miss me, partner?" Nico stretched his head and took a sniff of Glorieta's neck. "What is that scent? Tell me the name of the perfume so I can buy some for my mom."

The smell of alcohol on Nico's breath made her want to gag. "I'll have to check the name and let you …" Glorieta stopped in mid-sentence as Manuelito pedaled by on his bike. "You know what? Hop in the car, partner. I have a job for you that will give you enough cash to buy perfume for all your family members."

An Unexpected Proposal

The next morning, Fabiana found her mother in the kitchen, brewing coffee.

"Manuelito must have left early for school," Pearl said. "Didn't even have breakfast."

"He's probably taking pictures of the sunrise, Mom. He's quite the photographer. I'm impressed."

"Me too. Do you want me to go to the hospital with you?" Pearl asked.

"No. I'll call you and let you know how Johnny is doing."

When Fabiana walked into Johnny's room, he was asleep. She was surprised to see Carole already there. Fabiana's gaze shifted to the medical device flashing Johnny's vital signs and the intravenous tube delivering fluids into his body.

A man entered the room, holding a cup of coffee.

"Hello. Fabiana? Carole?"

"Yes," Fabiana said. "How do you know?"

"Your visitor badges. Besides, my son has been talking about the two of you. He will be happy to see you. I'm Joao."

"You're Johnny's father," Fabiana said. "Pleased to meet you. Johnny said you are an arborist,"

"That's right."

"What's wrong with Johnny?" Carole asked.

Fabiana looked at her and turned to Joao.

"I'm afraid he is not in good shape." Joao's mouth trembled, and he looked away for a moment. "My son was in remission. But the leukemia has returned and now he needs a bone marrow transplant right away. I'm not compatible. But I put myself in the donor bank for any potential match that needs a transplant."

"Leukemia?" Fabiana and Carole asked in unison, identical expressions of shock on their faces.

"He's suffered from nose bleeds for years, but yesterday's episode was the worst. Johnny was diagnosed with it when you were in Rio studying. Chemo made it somewhat better, but it has returned."

"Oh, my Lord." Fabiana picked up Johnny's left hand and watched him breathe in and out.

Johnny opened his eyes. "Am I in the presence of angels?" He managed a faint smile.

"How are you?" Both girls asked at the same time.

"Angel C.," Johnny said, looking at Carole. "Angel Bee," he said, turning to Fabiana. Did you meet my father? Did he tell you what the doctor said?"

"I know, Honey. Everything will be alright," Carole said.

"Yes. We'll make sure you have the best treatment, okay?"

The doctor, followed by the nurse, entered the room and checked Johnny's vitals.

"Doc, I feel miserable. Please tell me what to expect."

"We are searching for compatible bone marrow donors, Johnny. With a transplant, the prognosis is in your favor."

"But if you can't find a donor? How long, doc?"

"Johnny, we will find a donor. Don't stress out, okay?" Fabiana said.

"Doc, how long?" Johnny insisted.

"Three, six months. But we are doing all we can to find a suitable donor."

"Son, I'm counting on you to give me grandchildren and stay around to raise them," Joao teased.

After the doctor left, followed by the nurse, Fabiana took Johnny's hand again. "Is there anything I can do for you?"

"Yes, anything, honey?" Carole asked and took his other hand.

Fabiana was surprised. She didn't think Carole knew Johnny that well. What was going on?

Johnny's eyes were locked on Fabiana. "I don't want to die, Bee. I mean, I don't want to die a single man. Would you marry me?"

Sensing the urgency in his voice, Fabiana didn't know what to do. She didn't have the heart to say no to a dying man. "Right now, you need to rest. Gosh, I'm thirsty. Does anybody want anything from the cafeteria?"

Joao said he could use another cup of coffee and would go with her. He grabbed his bag and followed Fabiana.

Carole decided her mom must be correct—Fabiana had no interest in marrying Johnny. But if she, Carole, could entice him to marry her, she'd inherit his belongings, including a TV.

'I can't live if living is without you,' she sang in her off-key, squeaky voice.

Johnny's brows furrowed, and he turned towards the machines to check on his vitals. "Honey, if Fabiana won't marry you, I'll fulfill your dreams." Carole raised her hands. I'll need two rings because the ring finger on my right hand is slimmer. Okay?"

Johnny reached for her hands and kissed the ring finger on each. "Angel C."

Carole couldn't wait to tell her mother that she was going to inherit a TV. She would get a VCR, too. "I can't live, I can't live anymore."

Johnny's face contorted in pain. "Please, call the nurse."

***

In the cafeteria, Joao took a manila envelope from his bag and put it on his lap. "Fabiana, you know my ex-wife, Glorieta?"

"I do."

"I have to give her this envelope, and I don't want to leave it with Johnny. Would you please give it to her when you see her?"

Fabiana nodded and took the envelope from Joao. The outside was labeled: 'From Joao to Glorieta.'

"Wait a minute, I need to sign one more doc." He took a document from his bag and signed it. Then handed it to Fabiana to put it inside the envelope.

Fabiana glanced at the signature line. "I don't want to pry, but I'm afraid they misspelled your name."

"No. That's my legal name."

"Joao P. Iva? Shouldn't it be Joao Paiva?"

"No, it's John P. Iva. Joao Paiva is the Brazilian equivalent. It's easier to use Paiva when I'm down here."

Fabiana thought for a moment. "Excuse me. I have to make a phone call." She rose from her seat, went outside and located the nearest phone. Dropping the coins, her heart skipped a beat. She told herself she was calling for a good cause. But now she was flooded with doubt. She was about to hang up when the familiar voice on the other side said, "Hello."

"Paolo? It's me, Fabiana. How are you doing?"

"Fine, thanks."

"What's the name of the person you are looking for?"

"John P. Iva. Why?"

"Would you like to speak to him?"

"No way."

"Would you?"

Surprised, Paolo said, "Wait a minute. Okay. Put him on."

"I have to get him. Don't go anywhere. I'll call you right back."

Joao returned to Johnny's floor and entered his room in time to hear his son's voice.

"Nurse Mary, is there a notary public in this hospital?" Johnny asked.

"Another patient just requested one. Would you like to speak with her when she's free?"

"Please."

Fabiana found Joao in Johnny's room. Carole had scooted her chair closer to the bed and was holding Johnny's hand.

Fabiana smiled at all of them. She wanted to tell Joao about Paolo but was interrupted by a knock at the door.

A short middle-aged woman entered the room with a metallic case. "Did you request a notary, sir?

Fabiana couldn't believe how much the notary public looked like Glorieta. They had the same body shape and the same hairstyle. Save for the black hair color, the lab coat, and softer mascara, Fabiana would say this woman and Glorieta could be twins.

"Do you officiate weddings?" Johnny asked.

Fabiana was speechless. She looked from Carole to Johnny, wondering what was going on. Carole beamed. Johnny's dead-fish eyes met Fabiana's defiantly. *Bee. I don't want to die as a single man.*

"I do," the notary said. "But I don't have the proper documentation at the moment."

"Do you have a business card?" Joao asked. "I'll call you and make an appointment. Thank you for coming."

"Fabiana," Johnny asked. "Will you phone Ceeda?"

"Sure. What do you need?"

"Ask her to bring me a blue box that is in the top drawer of my dresser."

"Sure. I'll call her right now. Joao, would you come with me?"

"A friend of mine needs to speak with you," Fabiana told Joao as they walked down the hall.

A Long-Awaited Reunion

Paolo thought of the picture of his deceased mother in his Grandmother's living room. Raised by his grandparents, he never knew who his dad was. After his Grandfather died peacefully in his sleep, Paolo went through boxes of mementos and found his mother's diary. He hired a P.I. who had indicated the person he was looking for was in Rio de Janeiro and a few months later indicated the person might have gone from Rio de Janeiro to Jungle City.

Now, pacing in his living room, Paolo didn't know what to say to the man Fabiana had discovered. He jumped when the phone rang, and his heart began to race. What if it wasn't him?

"Hello, this is Joao. Fabiana said you wanted to speak with me. Do I know you?"

"No, you don't know me. But you may know Caroline Sendas?"

"Who?"

"1955, Boston, Caroline…"

"Oh. That Caroline. How is she doing?"

"You don't know?"

"Know what?"

"Caroline died in 1955." There was a significant pause, so Paolo asked, "Hello, are you there?"

"I'm here. I really didn't know. I'm sorry to hear that."

"She mentioned your name. She said you were her boyfriend. And..." Paolo paused, unsure of what to say next. "I'm her son. In her diary, she indicated you never knew about me. Her letters to you were returned, undeliverable. I've been searching for you a long time. I met Fabiana in Rio. And, somehow, she found you."

"Are you telling me that you are my son?"

"No. I'm asking. Are you my father?"

"Oh my God."

"I'm sorry to spring this on you without warning. I don't want anything from you. I just need to know."

"It's not that. I feel terrible. Leaving Caroline pregnant. Leaving you. I had no idea. Listen, I'd like to meet. Where are you?"

"In Jungle City. How about you?"

"I'm at the hospital in Jungle City at the moment. I always told Caroline that if I ever had a son, he would be named Paolo. I can't believe this. I know this is going to sound strange, but would you be willing to take a blood test?"

Paolo thought John wanted to verify his paternity and said, "No problem. I can be there this afternoon."

***

Glorieta had no doubt that Joao would spend every moment he could with Johnny, leaving her free to luxuriate in bed and consider her next move.

Plan A: Sandy Lagoons Investment was no longer an option now that Monlevade was dead.

Plan B: the W-Day. Glorieta didn't think Fabiana, the brat, would marry her son.

Plan C: suing Pearl was off the table. Prestle explained she'd have to hurt herself to get any kind of award.

Glorieta was too much of a coward to purposely inflict pain on herself. She was furious with Prestle for claiming her ruined designer suit wasn't sufficient grounds for a lawsuit.

Glorieta rose from bed and poured herself a glass of whisky. She didn't want to go to the kitchen to get ice because she would have to face Ceeda. Glorieta couldn't take Ceeda's passive-aggressive reproach for neglecting Johnny at this crucial time in his life. She ate a few bonbons and washed them down with warm whisky. The combination burned her throat and left her momentarily dizzy.

"Cheers to Plan D. Rancho Santa Fabiana will be mine no matter how many plans I have to set in motion." She looked in the mirror, toasted, and gulped the rest of the whisky.

The ringing of the telephone sidetracked Glorieta's thoughts. She picked up the receiver, listened, and, rolling her eyes, said, "Hello. Oh! Hi Sophia. Thanks for calling me back."

"What do you want?" Madame Sophia asked.

"Johnny has leukemia. I don't think he's in a condition to marry anyone."

"Then it's time for Plan D."

"I set things in motion last night."

"Good. Are you following my instructions?"

"Yes. That drunk guy, Nico, appeared just when I needed him."

"Where is the boy?"

"Nico has him in that barn in Rancho Santa Fabiana.

"Take good care of him—no violence, you hear me? I gave Trevor's business card to Fabiana. Let's hope she enlists his help now."

***

Thrilled that she had found Joao for Paolo, Fabiana went outside to place a phone call to her mother.

Pearl was in hysterics. Fabiana had trouble understanding what she said. Eventually, she understood that Pearl had received a call from a man saying Manuelito had been kidnapped and warning her not to contact the police.

Fabiana remembered the business card Madame Sophia had given her. She retrieved it from her wallet. *The P.I. will help us.*

The phone rang at Trevor's house. Fabiana called right on schedule.

He listened to the frantic voice on the other side of the line. Not to arouse any suspicions, he asked, "And you said your name is…"

"Fabiana. I was referred to you by your cousin, Madame Sophia. My brother disappeared. We can't go to the police."

"Calm down. How old is your brother?" Trevor asked.

"Fifteen."

"When was he seen last?"

"Last night, he took his bike and never—"

"Where are you?"

"At the hospital."

"Did you say, hospital? Are you sick?

"No, I'm fine. I'm visiting a patient."

"Can we meet in 15 minutes?"

"Yes."

"Do you drive?"

"No. I mean, yes. But I don't have a car."

"I'll pick you up at the hospital parking lot, and we'll search for him."

"Do you charge by the hour?"

"Don't worry, please. First, let's find your brother."

***

"Fabiana just called," Trevor reported. "Cousin, you are truly a psychic. What's next?"

"Take Fabiana to the burned barn," Madam Sophia instructed. "Glorieta will meet you there. While you wait for her, here's what you'll do."

Trevor listened and then hung up.

Rubbing his hands, he decided he must be psychic, too, as he foresaw lots of money in his bank account.

The Unforeseen Bond

While maneuvering the car into the hospital parking garage, Paolo saw Fabiana enter a vehicle and leave the premises. Paolo entered the lobby and looked around, wondering why she didn't stick around to say hello. One man was facing the door, an anxious look on his face. Paolo walked up to him and offered his hand. "Joao?" They greeted each other warmly, and Joao got a good look at Paolo's ear. Joao believed ears were an excellent way to tell if someone was related.

"Let's have a seat for a moment," Joao said, indicating a group of chairs.

After they took their seats, Joao looked Paolo in the eyes. "I didn't mention this on the phone, but I have another son. He's dying of leukemia."

"I'm so sorry." Paolo did feel sorry for the man. He looked like a nice guy.

"Are you still willing to take a blood test?" Joao asked.

"Let's do it."

"Paolo, this is a lot to ask. We need a test to see if you are compatible with my other son. He needs a bone marrow transplant."

"Whoa! I thought you wanted a paternity test."

"Will you take the blood test, please? And decide later whether you want to be a donor or not?"

Paolo could see that Joao was desperate.

"What would that entail?"

"The doctor can tell you more."

After the nurse collected the vials of blood, the doctor came over to speak with Paolo. He listened. "Siblings are most likely to be a match," the doctor said.

With mixed emotions, Paolo met Joao's eyes. Paolo didn't even know for sure that Joao was his father. Now, he was being asked to undergo this risky medical procedure for a brother he never knew he had.

Joao made it clear that it was Paolo's choice.

Paolo felt powerful and terrified at the same time. The doctor was waiting for an answer.

"If you are compatible, we would take stem cells from the marrow in your hip."

"How?" Paolo asked.

"We use long needles under general anesthesia. The procedure usually takes one to two hours."

"Any side effects?" Joao and Paolo asked simultaneously.

"The most common are back or hip pain, fatigue and bruising at the incision site," the doctor said.

Paolo wasn't worried about complications. It was more a question of undertaking the responsibility of saving the life of a man who could turn out to be his step-brother. He didn't know anything about these people. But there was precious little time to become acquainted. He looked upward. "In memory of my mother - I would have saved her if I could - it's worth the risk."

"Your mother was a beautiful soul, Paolo," Joao said. "I wish things were different. But I know she would be very proud of you."

After the nurse took Paolo's blood, the doctor shook Paolo's hand and patted Joao on the shoulder. "I'll be in touch the moment we get the results."

Joao turned to his son. He had no doubt Paolo was his son. This young American was full of compassion. "Thank you so much. How about a bite to eat? The cafeteria here is good."

They took their trays to a quiet table in the corner of the cafeteria. Paolo put ketchup in the fries and asked, "Why did you leave the U.S. without a trace?"

Joao chewed and swallowed a bite of hamburger. "I wasn't trying to hide. The local people changed the spelling of my name to Joao Paiva. I can only guess that any letters addressed to John

P. Iva didn't find me because I moved to Jungle City, and your mother would have thought I was in Rio…"

"I get it. Okay. Would you have believed my mother if she told you she was pregnant?"

"I loved her. I would have done the right thing."

Done the right thing. The words resonated in Paolo's mind. What did *doing the right thing* mean, anyway?

Later, they met the doctor in the corridor outside of Johnny's room. The test results indicated that Paolo was a compatible donor.

That was enough for Joao. He hugged Paolo and said, "Son."

Paolo made the thumbs-up sign and said, "Let me meet my step-brother."

***

Carole looked at Johnny peacefully napping, and left the hospital. The door opened, and Joao entered the room talking with Paolo.

"Hi, Dad. Where is the bride?" Johnny asked as soon as he opened his eyes.

"Wait a sec, Johnny. I'm sure she'll be back soon. I was hoping you could meet your step-brother Paolo. He's come from America to save you."

"What do you mean?"

"He's a match, Johnny." Joao beamed. "And he's agreed to be your donor."

"I didn't know I had a step-brother."

"Neither did I," Paolo said. "We have a lot to catch up on. How are you doing?"

I feel better already, knowing I have a donor. My bride will be here soon. If you are my step-brother, then you'll love her."

Trevor asked Fabiana a few questions. "Teenagers! Do you know his friends?"

"My mother called every parent from the school."

"Any favorite place he likes to go to?"

"Yes. He likes to ride his bike to my ranch."

That was a lucky break. Trevor already knew how to get there, but he asked Fabiana for directions to avoid raising suspicions.

"The ranch is our first stop," he said.

"Why didn't my mother and I think of that?" Fabiana wondered.

"That's why you need a private investigator like yours truly," he said. At the ranch, Trevor parked his car under a tree where it couldn't be seen from the entrance. He picked up a bag with food, a blanket, and four water bottles. He explained Manuelito might be hungry or hurt and they needed to be prepared.

"This is a big place," Fabiana said. "I don't know where to begin." She looked down at her fancy flip-flops, then around at the jungle and tried to suppress her fear.

Trevor put his free hand on her arm. "Quiet. We don't want to alert anyone until we know what's happening here."

Fabiana nodded and turned down the trail leading to the barn.

A caiman emerged from the bushes and entered the swampy water surrounding the barn's backside. Fabiana stopped to watch it, wishing she had a tranquilizing gun.

Trevor pounced and covered her face with a chloroform-soaked cloth. After a brief struggle, Fabiana fell lifeless in his arms.

Trevor carried her to the barn and laid her on the ground outside. Manuelito was half-asleep, tied to a pillar in the middle of the room. Squatting and looking concerned, Trevor tapped the boy's face. "Manuelito," Trevor asked, faking compassion. "Who did this to you?"

"A drunk guy named Nico and that weirdo, Glorieta. Please untie me, man," Manuelito begged.

Trevor stood up and went behind the pillar. Sensing the man was taking too long to untie him, Manuelito asked, "Who are you? Are you with them? Answer me?"

Trevor didn't bother replying. Instead, he asked,

"Are you thirsty?"

"Untie me."

Trevor didn't move, and Manuelito asked, "Who are you?"

"Hungry? Trevor unwrapped a sandwich and fed Manuelito. After the sandwich was gone, he opened a water bottle for himself and drank the entire bottle. "Thirsty, boy? Last chance."

Manuelito nodded and let Trevor pour water into his mouth.

Trevor pulled another chloroform-soaked cloth from his bag and placed it on Manuelito's face. After the boy lost consciousness, he carried Fabiana inside. He braced her listless body on a wobbly chair facing the pillar, tying her hands behind her. "I can't wait to see this brat's reaction when she wakes up."

Glorieta parked next to Trevor's car and approached the barn in high heels. Furious that the dirt and bushes were damaging her expensive shoes and manicure irreparably, she opened the barn door and demanded water.

Trevor threw her a bottle. "Catch."

The water fell by her feet. "Gee. Thanks, cousin. Still your unmannered self, I see. Gosh, I can't believe Sophia would make us come all the way out here in this unbearable heat. But I don't mind. You know why?"

"I don't need to be a psychic to say you will be rewarded with a sizable fortune."

"Exactly. Today is the day that my dream comes true. Rancho Santa Fabiana will finally be mine."

"Wait a minute. Sophia said one-third of the ranch would be mine."

Glorieta took a deep breath. *Dream on, criatura,* "Sophia will give you your part. Don't worry. We are a team."

"You never paid me for all the time I spent trying to locate Monlevade's tube of blueprints."

"You didn't get paid because you never delivered."

Fabiana started to wake up but, recognizing Glorieta's voice decided to remain motionless. She heard the high heels stomping around her chair. Squinting her eyes, she saw her brother lying awkwardly before her. She stifled a cry. Was he hurt?

Glorieta opened her Chanel purse and retrieved her copy of the deed. She asked Trevor for a pen.

"I don't have one."

"How will this brat sign without a pen?" Complaining that she had to return to her car to get a pen in her glove compartment, that she was going to ruin her heels walking back and forth in that unforgiving dirt, and that she had to do everything herself, Glorieta left the barn, but changed her mind as soon as she was outside.

"Trevor," Fabiana said as soon as Glorieta left. "Untie us, please. I promise to give you more than they promised you."

"He will do no such thing, you brat." Glorieta stood in the doorway. "It occurs to me that you might have a pen in your purse." She pointed to Fabiana's purse carelessly thrown in a corner of the room. Fanning herself, Glorieta said, "More water, Trevor."

"Why are you doing this to us? We always treated you nicely." Fabiana said.

"Her brother called you a weirdo, Glorieta," Trevor said.

"What do you want from us?"

"Isn't it obvious?" Glorieta stood in front of Fabiana. "The hermit promised…"

"Hermit?"

"Fabiana, please don't interrupt me when I'm talking," Glorieta said, "Your grandpa! That's how I call him. He took advantage of my cousin."

Fabiana looked around the barn, searching for answers in the dark shadows.

"The hermit sent you to Campo Grande to tell her, forget…"

"Madam Sophia? We never knew what Grandfather meant. Forget what?"

"His promises. He got her started as a model. He arranged for her to appear in a *Simca Chambord* magazine ad. It's hanging in her hallway."

"Madam Sophia said an ex-fiancé got her that gig."

"That was your grandfather, the hermit. She told him that the gig didn't help her career take off, that she was alone and needed to plan for the future. He said he had no living relatives either and was considering leaving the ranch to someone - he just didn't know who.

"But interesting enough, he gave Sophia an envelope to keep safe. Inside was the ranch deed. Wouldn't you think he was giving the deed to her? He said he didn't have any living relatives and asked her to keep the deed to the ranch for him.

"She decided to hide the deed here, thinking it would be the safest place, but the ranch burned down, and the hermit spent years in the hospital. As soon as Sophia learned that he was dying, she asked me to get a replacement deed signed over to her. I became his caregiver, mentioned Sophia's name and told him she hadn't forgotten. He nodded, so I thought he was agreeing, but he died before he could sign the deed over. The ranch was technically in my hands."

"All of our hands," Trevor interjected.

"Quiet. Don't you interrupt me when I'm talking," Glorieta aimed her furious eyes in Trevor's direction, then rolled her eyes toward Fabiana with the same fury. "Next thing I know, you guys show up out of nowhere. He tells me the woman holding his hand is his daughter, Pearl, and that you are the spitting image of his late wife. He announced he would leave the ranch to you, and you could not sell it until you were married."

Fabiana furrowed her eyebrows. She could hear her grandfather's voice: *The ranch is yours, but only tell after you get married.* He clearly said tell, not sell.

Glorieta looked at her wristwatch. "Trevor, it's almost time. Nico is coming over to feed Manuelito. Be ready with the chloroform."

Fabiana tried to loosen the ropes around her wrists.

"Trevor, a pen."

"I told you I don't have a pen."

"Find me a pen in her bag, *criatura*. The brat will sign the deed even if she needs to sign it with blood. One way or the other, I'll have her sign with your blood if we can't find a pen."

The Search

Ceeda walked the hospital corridor, looking for Johnny's room. The door was ajar. With a gentle smile on her tired face, she made her way toward Johnny.

"Ceeda," Johnny said.

"Johnny. How are you doing? Our Lord is showering you with blessings."

"Thank you so much. Please sit. I miss your cooking."

"I brought you mashed potatoes, but the nurses confiscated them at the desk. They said you can't eat because you're having a procedure tomorrow. What are they going to do to you?" She gently patted his hand.

Johnny relayed the news about his transplant procedure and revealed his amazement in finding out that his step-brother was a suitable donor.

Ceeda listened and dabbed at her eyes with a tissue. "Didn't I say you were blessed? How else to explain this half-brother showing up in your hour of need? I'm looking forward to meeting him." She patted his hands and got up. "I'm going grocery shopping. What can I get you?"

"Potatoes. The first thing I want to do after leaving here will be to eat some of your famous mashed potatoes. You are the best. Thanks for coming. Hey, wait. Did you bring the ring box?"

"Yes. Here you are."

Johnny reached for the box and opened the lid. "It's empty."

"That's how I found it, not in your room, but in Glorieta's. No matter what, thank the Lord, Johnny," Ceeda said. "You'll soon come home and find the ring."

"I sure will," Johnny said.

When Joao arrived, Johnny asked him to pick up Carole and bring her to the hospital. He gave Joao Fabiana's address and explained she'd show him where Carole lived.

***

Pearl sat by the phone, hoping to hear from Manuelito. When Joao knocked on the door, Pearl yanked it open, filled with desperate hope. But she didn't recognize the man and struggled to hide her disappointment.

The man smiled tentatively. "I'm Joao Paiva, Johnny's father."

"Oh. Yes. Sorry to hear Johnny's ill."

"Is Fabiana in?" Joao asked.

"No," Pearl stifled a sob. "She's looking for her brother. He—he's missing—" Pearl could not hold the tears back. She didn't know what to do. She was terrified to go to the police and terrified Manuelito would be hurt.

"What's happened," Joao asked. "How can I help?"

Pearl saw the car parked in front of her house. "Is that your Jeep?"

Joao nodded. "Yes. Do you need a ride?"

"Please. I need a ride to Rancho Santa Fabiana."

Johnny was waiting for Joao and Carole back at the hospital. But Pearl seemed desperate. Joao had no idea what was going on, but Fabiana was Johnny's friend, and this family obviously needed help.

As Joao closed the car door after she took the passenger's seat, Pearl thought Joao looked like a gentleman, not the monster Glorieta painted whenever she referred to her ex-husband.

***

Manuelito opened his eyes and saw his sister making a silent, shushing sound with her lips. He closed his eyes and struggled to reach the end of the rope encircling his wrist.

Nico pushed open the door to the barn, whistling under his breath. Glorieta had promised to pay him today. He removed his baseball cap and looked around. His eyes widened in surprise when

148

he spotted Fabiana, then stepped backward when a man he didn't know approached. He looked at Glorieta with a puzzled look. Trevor put an arm on Nico's shoulder and grinned. "Good to meet you, man. I'm Glorieta's cousin. Thanks for helping out the ladies."

"Glad to be of service anytime-"

Trevor brought up his other hand and applied a chloroform-soaked cloth to Nico's face. After a brief struggle, Nico's body relaxed. Trevor laid him down next to Fabiana and looked around for something to tie him up with.

"Use his shirt, *criatura*," Glorieta snapped impatiently.

Fabiana could smell the sweat and booze seeping out of Nico's pores.

After tying Nico's hands behind his back, Trevor rolled him near Manuelito.

Fabiana had seen enough. "Help!" she screamed.

Manuelito struggled against his bonds.

"Someone help!" Fabiana repeated.

"Scream all you want, you brat! No one will hear you," Glorieta said.

The Rescue And The Jaguar

The first thing Joao and Pearl saw when they drove up to the ranch was Glorieta's Mercedes. "What's Glorieta doing here?" Pearl asked.

They looked at each other and climbed out of the Jeep. Joao looked around. The ranch was overgrown with dried trees. He opened the glove compartment, pulled out his tranquilizer gun, and slipped it in his belt. Then he motioned to Pearl to follow the footprints on the ground. As they approached the barn, they heard Fabiana's disturbing cry.

Joao held a finger to his lips before he removed the tranquilizer gun from his belt and, shielding Pearl behind him, advanced quietly toward the back of the barn. The back door was slightly ajar. Joao peeked through the narrow opening and saw three people turned so their backs were to him. Glorieta and a slim, bald man were on either side of Fabiana. Fabiana was seated and appeared to be struggling against them. With growing concern, Joao noticed two boys - one tied to a pillar and the other lying on the ground.

Pearl patted Joao on the shoulder, wanting to know what he was seeing. He shook his head to warn her to be still.

The boy tied to the pillar opened his eyes and croaked, "Water."

The bald man grunted, yanking Fabiana's arm. "You'll have to wait," the man shouted to Manuelito.

"Water," Manuelito repeated hoarsely, followed by a cough.

"Give the stupid kid some water," Glorieta shouted. "Sophia asked us not to hurt them." She rolled her shoulders and pasted a phony smile on her face. "You see, Fabiana, we are not barbarians. What would you prefer? Marry my son? Then, you can "dispose" of your property. Or sign these papers?"

"I'm afraid it's too late. Johnny is in the hospital dying…"

"Nobody dies from a bloody nose," Glorieta snapped.

"He wants to get married before he dies, and Carole graciously agreed," Fabiana lied.

"You gotta be kidding."

"They might already be married by now," Fabiana said, struggling against the man's hold on her wrist.

"What an idiot. I'll deal with him later." Glorieta said, "I'm going to ask you nicely one more time. Be good and sign this paper." She shook the paper in front of Fabiana but the girl refused to even look at it. "In that case, Trevor, make Manuelito drink chloroform instead of water."

Pearl gasped and whispered, "Manuelito is my son." Joao moved his palms down to calm her. Pearl nodded and took a deep breath.

The bald man finished knotting Fabiana's restraints and grinned at Glorieta. He grabbed a glass bottle and stood in front of Manuelito.

"No, Trevor," Fabiana screamed. "I'll sign it."

Manuelito shook his head. "No, Fabiana, don't."

Trevor squatted in front of Manuelito. The boy's fist shot up and caught him under his chin. Trevor tumbled back and collapsed.

Joao nodded at Pearl, and they rushed through the door. Glorieta wrapped her hands around Fabiana's neck. The girl struggled, gasping for air. Pearl screamed.

Joao pulled his tranquilizing gun, pointed it at Glorieta, and told her to release Fabiana. He heard a scuffle behind him and turned just as Trevor slammed against his arm, making him drop the gun.

Joao rammed his fist into Trevor's solar plexus. The thin man hunched in pain and pulled a knife from his boot. They circled one another until Joao lunged, grabbing Trevor's wrist. Despite Trevor's small size, he overpowered Joao and waggled the knife inches from Joao's face. Manuelito intervened by hitting Trevor in the head with a chair. Trevor fell back with a grunt, unconscious. Joao pushed himself up and asked Manuelito to tie Trevor up.

Pearl grabbed the chloroform-soaked cloth Trevor had prepared for Manuelito and held it in front of Glorieta's face. "Let my daughter go."

"She has to sign this paper first."

"What paper?"

"The deed to the ranch," Fabiana elevated her voice. "Glorieta wants me to sign it over to her."

"Glorieta, she can't sign anything. She can't even sell it. The ranch isn't hers yet," Pearl lied. "Besides, I have the original deed at home."

Nico stirred, drawing Pearl's attention. "What's he doing here?"

Joao shook his head in exasperation. "Glorieta, this is insane. Our son is in the hospital with acute leukemia, and you're trying to steal this girl's property? Let her go."

"Hey, untie me this instant," Nico urged.

Manuelito untied the shirt from Nico's arms. Before anyone could react, Nico twisted Manuelito's arm behind his back.

"No one is signing anything until I get my money. I kidnapped this boy, and I'm going to be paid," Nico said.

"How much to let him go?" Pearl asked, opening her purse.

"Three hundred and fifty dollars."

Pearl's face fell. "I don't have that much on me."

Joao pulled out his wallet and handed Nico the cash. Pearl started to protest, but Joao shook his head.

Nico pushed Manuelito forward before turning on Glorieta. "Don't think you'll get away with double-crossing me." He grabbed his shirt, lit a cigarette without listening to Joao's protest, and ran outside.

Joao, Pearl, and Manuelito circled around Glorieta.

At that moment, a loud shuffling noise ricocheted outside the barn, catching everyone's attention. Fabiana jerked her head upwards and hit Glorieta's chin. Joao grabbed Glorieta's wrists and forced them away from Fabiana's head. Pearl pressed the chloroform-soaked fabric onto Glorieta's nose and only released it when Glorieta was motionless in Joao's arm. They tied her hands with Joao's belt.

Pearl threw her arms around her son. "Thank goodness you're okay." She and Manuelito untied Fabiana and helped her stand up. "Let's get you both home and have a nice dinner. I'll make your favorite heart of palm pie."

The last rays of sunset entering the barn soon gave way to a dark sky. The shuffling sound in the trees grew louder outside.

"That's odd," Joao said, sticking his head out the window. "The tuiuius never fly once they've settled for the night." Joao stiffened, "That stupid boy might have started a fire with his cigarette! Let's get out of here."

Joao and Pearl carried Glorieta, and Manuelito and Fabiana dragged Trevor out of the barn. The air was dry and hot. Joao pulled a pair of binoculars from his vest pocket. "Through the swamp. I see a boat there."

They rushed towards the water. And froze. A caiman stood between them and the rowboat. Its open mouth displayed a lethal set of teeth. Pearl looked backward and said, "We can't get back to your Jeep." Flames engulfed the trees and advanced on the barn. Joao asked the group not to make sudden movements. To steer clear of the caiman, they veered a few yards to the left, and Joao instructed everyone to sprint in a straight line. He and Pearl shuffled Glorieta into the back of the boat.

Fabiana heard a seesaw sound off to her right, stepped backward and looked up. A jaguar was leaping from branch to branch, trying to flee the flames. Fabiana transferred the unconscious Trevor to Manuelito and, shielding her brother, faced the feline with curious eyes. Her late grandfather's advice flashed in her mind, "Look larger than the animal." Fearless, she raised her arms above her head and braced for the worst. The jaguar pounced. Fabiana felt the wind dance around her body.

Joao raised the tranquilizing gun, but the jaguar landed on the caiman. The reptile trashed and snapped but couldn't get its long head around to bite the jaguar. Its tail beat against the swamp's water to no avail. Stunned, Fabiana met the jaguar's gaze as it ran away with its prey. She had to be yanked into the boat. Joao helped her and Manuelito lift Trevor into the boat. Joao and Fabiana grabbed the oars and pulled away from the fire.

Pearl watched Glorieta regain consciousness. "I can't believe you kidnapped my son and tried to force my daughter to give you Rancho Santa Fabiana." Glorieta looked away, refusing to meet her eyes.

They pulled to shore on the outskirts of town, and Fabiana found a phone booth to call the police.

Unintended Consequences

At the police station, Glorieta and Trevor were each allowed one phone call. Glorieta called Prestle and was told that he had collapsed at the office and was sedated at the hospital. Trevor called Madame Sophia in Campo Grande.

"So? Are we the happy owners of the ranch?" she asked. There was a knock at her front door. "Hang on." The long cord of the phone allowed her to carry it with her. She pulled open the door to find three police officers showing their badges. One of the officers shoved a summons in her face at the very moment Trevor was screaming that he and Glorieta needed bail money as fast as possible. "Not in a million years," Sophia said before slamming the receiver down. Handcuffed and defeated, she was escorted to the police car.

In Jungle City, after taking their depositions, the police offered Joao and Fabiana's family a ride. Exhausted from the ordeal, they rode in silence to Pearl's house. Wrapping her arms around Manuelito, mother and son entered their home. Joao asked Fabiana for Carole's address. "I must apologize that I was supposed to give her a ride to the hospital earlier today."

"She lives around the block. I'll take you there," Fabiana said.

Fabiana walked with Joao, thanking him profusely for his rescue efforts.

"I did what anyone would have done. I'm so sorry my ex-wife has endangered your family in this way. I don't know what got into her."

Fabiana nodded, thinking Joao was much nicer than Glorieta ever let on. Of course, Glorieta was much worse than she ever let on. Fabiana shuddered at the thought of the woman badgering her poor, helpless grandfather.

"Look," Joao said. "Don't tell Johnny what Glorieta did."

Fabiana looked up in surprise.

"At least, not right away. I don't want him going into surgery worrying about his mother."

Rounding the corner, Fabiana agreed. They both stopped at the same time. Joao's Jeep was parked in front of Carole's house.

Carole opened the door before they knocked. In a fake teasing tone of voice, she asked where they'd been.

Joao asked for his car keys.

"Your car? What are you talking about?" Carole asked.

"That Jeep is my car," Joao answered. "Some kid named Nico stole it today."

"What?" Carole's eyes widened. "My brother?"

"That delinquent is your brother?" Joao asked.

"The police will soon arrest him," Fabiana said.

"Because of this car? Joao, please tell the police there's no harm done, promise me? Now, can you give me a ride to see Johnny?"

The key was still in the ignition. Joao drove Fabiana and Carole to the hospital. He dropped them off before he went home to freshen up. He promised to come back later and give the girls a ride home.

When they entered his room, Johnny apologized to Fabiana for pressuring her to marry him. At the same time, he had feelings for Carole.

Carole smiled and nudged Fabiana out of the way, taking Johnny's hand with a proprietary smile.

"You don't have to apologize for anything," Fabiana said.

"It was my mom's idea. She said I'd get a promotion if I were married."

Carole looked at Johnny and said, "Are you serious?"

Johnny nodded and cradled Carole's hand in both of his.

Fabiana could see the love in their eyes as they gazed at one another. "I'm happy for you both. The sooner you get married, the better. I told your mom you had already married Carole."

"Great. Then, Prestle will promote me. But, Bee, there's one thing I need to tell you. I have the drawings."

"What drawings?"

"Remember the man who drowned in the pond on your property in December? He left blueprints for a resort called Rancho Santa Fabiana with my mother. My mother brought them into the bank and left them in the conference room. I found them and thought they were yours, so I put them in my desk drawer. My mother turned herself into a tornado trying to find them. But, by rights, they belong to you. If you ever decide to develop your property, you might want to use those plans."

"Thank you. I've had the most wonderful idea. I'm going to build a wildlife rehabilitation center, a sanctuary... a Jaguar sanctuary. Please, Johnny, get well soon."

"I will, thanks to Paolo's generous blood marrow donation."

"Where is he?" Fabiana asked.

"Filling out some paperwork. He told me how he met you in Rio. He'll be here soon. I can't believe how much he reminds me of Dad. They both have the biggest hearts I know."

When Paolo returned, he asked Fabiana if she would go with him to the cafeteria. She gladly obliged.

Carole asked Johnny to turn the TV on. Her soap opera was beginning. Holding hands, they watched the chapter that, surprisingly enough, was about a father and son's reconnection and the story behind the son's name.

"Veronica Luz, the actress playing the doctor, is my mother's cousin," Carole said. Veronica was explaining that she loved the Rosetta Stone and had named Ollion, hoping that one day Champ would learn about their son. Now, Champ was visiting Ollion in the hospital. With tears streaming down her face, the doctor exclaimed, "My Champollion!" The three characters embraced. The scene cut to ancient Egypt where Champollion, the decipherer of Egyptian hieroglyphs and a founding figure in the field of Egyptology, was examining the writings in the Rosetta Stone...

"Honey…"

"Yes, Angel C."

"Do you know why I like soap operas?"

"Why?"

"Because the stories mirror real life perfectly and always have happy endings. I wanna cry."

"Let's make sure those are happy tears. Will you marry me?"

"Yes! And as I sang before, *I can't live if…*"

"Here, put your head on my shoulder and cry all you want, Angel C."

A Promise and New Beginnings

Paolo bought Fabiana a cold bottle of *Guarana* in the hospital cafeteria and sat beside her. "How have you been? I missed you."

"I missed you too. Thank you for being there for Johnny."

"Is he an important friend?"

"Yes." Fabiana tried to stifle a huge yawn.

"You look exhausted."

"It's been quite a day."

"Tell me about it."

"Now? It's a long story. I just want to take a long shower and get some sleep."

Paolo relished the fragrance in the air as he took her hand, gently kissing her palm. A tingling sensation flowed through Fabiana's body as their eyes engaged in a captivating gaze.

Joao and Carole entered the cafeteria. "You ready to go home?" he asked Fabiana.

Fabiana looked at Paolo. His eyes morphed into the eyes of the jaguar. She kissed him on the corner of his lips and wished him the best of luck on his surgery. The delicate texture of his lips and the enigmatic intensity in his jaguar-like eyes lingered vividly in Fabiana's thoughts all the way home.

The next morning, Pearl handed Fabiana a large piece of parchment. "This is the original deed of your property, darling."

As Fabiana unrolled it, a small note fell to the ground. "I never noticed that note in there. What does it say?" Pearl asked.

"Fabiana, please remember what I said to you. You can only tell you've inherited the ranch after you get married. Marry a man who loves you for yourself, not your property. Be happy! Blessings, your Grandfather."

"*Tell* – after you get married?" Pearl asked. "Not *sell*? All those years, we thought you couldn't sell until after you married."

Fabiana gave a big smile. "Actually, Mom, I'm glad we kept it in the family. Because now, with Joao's help, I intend to turn it into a sanctuary to protect the trees and the animals, especially the Jaguar. We've already started accumulating the funds for it."

***

The following day, the news crew from the Jungle City TV station came to Pearl's house to interview the family about their ordeal at Rancho Santa Fabiana.

Pearl asked the cameraman to set up his video camera in the living room. After reporter Marcia Passaredo prepped her for the informal talk, Pearl said she had something to show to the public and would be right back.

Fabiana arrived home in time to see her mother disappearing into the kitchen. Puzzled by the strangers in the living room, she followed her mother into the backyard.

"Isn't this exciting? Marcia Passaredo from Channel 8 News wants to interview us about our ordeal. I want to take advantage and announce my project," Pearl collected her plastic containers of sweet potato slips and other seeds and placed them on a tray.

***

Ula saw the Channel 8 News van pass by her house. She immediately closed the TV guide and followed the van to Pearl's house. After a quick knock on the open door, she stepped inside.

The cameraman zoomed in on her. "Testing, One, Two, Three."

Ula was confused and excited at the same time. Was the cameraman asking her to make a statement? With a big smile on her face, she told the cameraman that he was in the house of a saint. She dropped in because she wanted to thank Pearl for all the times she allowed her to watch TV, especially the soap opera where her cousin was the star. "You see," Ula said. "Our TV is locked in my son's room where we couldn't watch it. But I have good news for Pearl. I won't have to bother her anymore. I'll watch TV at my

160

son-in-law's house. I also wanted to tell her I'm so sorry her family was victimized by those horrible criminals, especially their terrible cousin."

Marcia motioned to the cameraman to keep rolling.

"My son is also a victim in this whole ordeal. I'm looking for an attorney to defend him. If you are watching, contact me."

Pearl and Fabiana reentered the living room carrying small plastic containers on a tray and stopped to listen to what Ula was saying. Fabiana whispered to Pearl, "What's Ula doing here?"

The reporter turned the microphone to Fabiana and said, "Fabiana, I understand you knew the kidnappers personally. Has that affected your sense of trust?" Marcia asked.

"I never realized people could be so manipulative and greedy," Fabiana said into the microphone. "Nonetheless, we were able to liberate ourselves. We are home, thankfully."

Ula squeezed between Fabiana and Pearl. "And this woman here, her mother, is a great cook."

The reporter ignored Ula and asked Fabiana, "How have the fires affected your property values?"

"My mom has a wonderful idea to restore the luxuriant foliage," Fabiana said, gently moving in front of Ula and putting her arm around Pearl's shoulders.

"Luxuriant." Ula smiled and made two thumbs up behind the mother and daughter.

"Tell her, Mom."

Pearl raised one of the paper cups in her hands. "We invite everyone to plant seeds in the burn area. Every catering order I fill will be accompanied by a paper cup with sprouted seeds that benefit the wildlife." The cameraman zoomed in on the containers.

"If you just joined us, we are live, speaking with the Grande family. The young boy, Manuelito, was kidnapped. But he is back home, thanks to Fabiana's rescue efforts. Is Manuelito available? May we ask him some questions?"

"Sorry. He's not available at the moment," Pearl said.

"We wouldn't have escaped without the heroic efforts of my mother, the arborist, Joao Paiva, and the resident jaguar," Fabiana said.

"A jaguar?"

Fabiana explained how the feline saved them all from the caiman.

The cameraman zoomed in on Fabiana's eyes.

"Wish I knew if the jaguar survived the fire," she concluded, looking directly into the camera.

"What an inspiring story! Thank you, ladies. Back to you at the studio."

Shopping Spree

Johnny eased out of bed and allowed Joao to help him dress. He looked at the flowers sent by the Grande family and his co-workers. There was nothing from Glorieta. "I wish Mother had come to see me in the hospital".

"Glorieta is not in a good place," Joao said softly. "We'll visit her as soon as you are strong enough."

"Where is she?"

Johnny had to sit down on the side of the bed when Joao told him Glorieta had been arrested for kidnapping. He was even more shocked when he learned she had kidnapped Fabiana's brother. Johnny stared at the ceiling. Images of peanut butter candies danced in the empty space before him.

A moment later, Carole pranced into the room, all smiles. "Are you ready to go home?" she asked. "Are you taking these flowers?"

While the nurse entered with a wheelchair, Johnny rose and leaned on Carole. "I already have the most special flower from the garden."

"Oh! Honey. Are you also a poet? But, these flowers are still fresh."

Johnny said he wanted to give one of the flower arrangements to Ceeda. Fabiana and Carole could divvy up the remaining baskets. Carole said, "Fabiana has too much to deal with right now. I'll just keep them all."

Joao drove Johnny and Carole to Glorieta's home. Ceeda greeted them with hugs and a feast—which included a huge platter of mashed potatoes. Afterward, Carole asked to see Johnny's bedroom.

She stood in the doorway. "Are you kidding me? No TV?"

"No, just the little one in my mother's bedroom."

"You don't watch soap opera?"

"Only when I go to Fabiana's house."

"Oh, honey. We are going on a shopping spree," Carole hugged and kissed him.

***

A short sound effect filled the airwaves. Mrs. Mae said on the radio microphone, "Dear listeners, I have some exciting updates! Fabiana will rock Jungle City with her fantastic artwork next week. It's not just about the art—it's a chance to support her family's vital reforestation efforts. You are invited to stop by and show some love!

"So, mark your calendars for next week's art extravaganza at Jungle City Bank! Carole pitched the idea to Johnny and Fabiana, and get this—she's keeping just ten percent of the sales to help bail her brother out of jail. And to make it even more remarkable, they're handing out Pearl's sweet potato slips and seed-filled containers at the exhibition.

"A special shoutout to Johnny, the newly appointed Vice President of the bank, for making things happen at the bank.

"Joao, Pearl, and Manuelito are in on the action, too. They're hauling Fabiana's jaw-dropping fish eyes and rosette patterns to the bank's conference room. Pearl is in charge of catering the event and giving the patrons small paper cups filled with sprouted seeds. The deal is simple: scatter those seeds in any burned area in the Pantanal.

"This whole thing is a real team effort, showing the community's unity. These people are together, fueled by art, activism, and a shared commitment to bringing the Pantanal back to life.

"I must add that the TV interview gave a boost to Pearl's business, and Jungle City citizens voted Pearl's catering the best in the region. And on this positive note, I wrap up my story today, dear listeners. Hey, on more thing. Make sure you stay updated on the jaguar's comeback. My sources say it's gonna be on national TV soon.

Thank you for being with me over these past few weeks. I appreciate you all." Mrs. Mae said as the music faded in the background, signaling the broadcast's conclusion.

July 1985 - The World Watches

Fabiana lay on the couch, drawing feline eyes. On the monochromatic TV in the corner of the room, the weatherman has predicted temperatures to reach the high 90s. Fabiana waved her sketchbook in front of her face, trying to counteract the unbearable heat in Jungle City.

A Breaking News alert filled the air. Fabiana closed her sketchbook and watched as images of bandaged paws appeared on the screen. She leaped off the couch, slipped into her tennis shoes, and grabbed a wrapped rectangular package leaning against the wall near the door. She wrote a note which she left on the table: *Mom, Any minute now. Hope you are watching the Breaking News* and ran out the door, leaving the TV on with the reporter saying, "Stay tuned. We will be bringing you updates as they happen live."

Fabiana looked around in vain to hail a taxi. Save for the symphony of crickets and birds in the air, the streets were still. She figured people were indoors not because of the heat but to witness the most awaited moment in Jungle City being broadcast live on national TV. Her heart pounded in her chest as she sprinted towards the bus stop. Not even half a block away, she saw her brother zooming towards her on his bicycle. "It's happening," she called to him. "We have to go to the ranch now!"

Manuelito roared and shouted over his shoulder, "Hop on, sis. Hold tight. We are gonna fly." He pedaled hard and fast, making the wheels of his bike lift up a dust cloud from the dirt and gravel road.

Pearl arrived home later. The TV was on. She read Fabiana's message and focused on the news. The image of the jaguar was replaced by a man in his mid-fifties. Pearl didn't need to read the name on the bottom of the screen.

"Our very own Joao Paiva," Pearl said.

Marcia Passaredo, the reporter, asked Joao if he was a veterinarian.

"No, once an arborist, always a preservationist. After the fires are contained, I am brought in to check on trees. Fortunately, my team came across this jaguar with third-degree burns on all four of his paws, under a Manduvi tree. We were able to hit it with tranquilizer darts and bring it to this place, where for the last couple of weeks, it has been treated and monitored for any signs of infection."

The moment the siblings hopped off the bicycle at Rancho Santa Fabiana, they raced over to the barn, where they lined up behind the TV crew. Fabiana's nails, adorned with a rosette pattern, gently tapped the glass enclosure, signaling a soft hello to Joao.

The cameraman captured the long-anticipated moment, allowing everyone present at the barn, as well as those watching from home, to witness the round, amber eyes of the jaguar slowly opening. Filled with joy, Fabiana felt an immense empathy for the jaguar that had endured so much suffering in the recent fires on her ranch.

"When will the jaguar return to its natural habitat?" Marcia Passaredo asked.

"At this point, it's too early to say. But it will receive the best possible care thanks to Fabiana Grande, the owner of Rancho Santa Fabiana and the founder of this state-of-the-art wildlife rehabilitation center in Jungle City."

Marcia approached Fabiana, asked her if she had any statements for the viewers at home, and passed her the microphone.

"I'm sorry that this jaguar had to endure such trauma due to the thoughtless act of one criminal," Fabiana replied with determination in her voice. "That is why I now resolve to stay in Jungle City. My ranch will now be a place of education and preservation for wildlife in the Pantanal region. I have chosen a new name for the property: *Like Jaguar Eyes.*" And with that, she unwrapped the rectangular package to reveal the plaque she had designed.

Facing the camera, Marcia said, "It's too soon to know when this feline will return to its natural environment. But thanks to this young woman's efforts, this jaguar will receive the best possible care."

Epilogue: Who's The Jaguar? Who's the Prey?

Paolo recovered from his procedure at Joao's house. Fabiana visited him often. Every day at sunset, they marveled at the flocks of birds flying overhead toward their nests in the Pink Ipe, Jacaranda, and other trees.

Shortly before Paolo was scheduled to return to the U.S., Fabiana invited him for dinner. She wore the silk blouse featuring a jaguar rosette pattern and the psychedelic skirt Paolo purchased for her in Rio de Janeiro. Slits in the midi skirt revealed enticing glimpses of the straps of the snake-shaped spiral stilettos swirling up her calves. She heard a knock at the front door and, filled with anticipation, glanced through the peephole. She opened the door, stepped outside and smiled.

Paolo took her hand, raised her hand above her head and twirled her around to admire her beauty. His whistle blended with the sound of tuiuius, blue macaws and white storks flying over the house.

"Beautiful, isn't it?" Fabiana said as they watched the birds. When the birds were far away in the distance, Fabiana and Paolo went to the backyard, where she opened a cooler and poured him a refreshing glass of *Guarana*.

He nodded his thanks and read the writing on the glass aloud, "From Here to Infinity."

"Yes," Fabiana said. "Since Johnny's near brush with death, I've been thinking a lot about the meaning of the words finite and infinite."

"Pardon?"

"You are leaving for the States soon. I'm searching for ways to make finite moments like this last for infinity."

Paolo furrowed his brow, momentarily perplexed.

"I have something for you," Fabiana took a container of sweet potato slips from a tray. "Here. This is what I mean. Let's make this finite moment become infinite by planting these slips for a brighter planet."

They crouched with the slips cradled in their hands and embedded them into the ground with their fingers. Their fingertips and gazes met, allowing for an intimate connection that gave a feeling of warmth and delight. The shared joy lingered in the air, creating a bond beyond the simple planting of slips.

As they stood, they turned toward each other.

"I'm considering staying in Jungle City," Paolo said, wrapping her tightly.

Fabiana felt his warm breath on her neck intoxicating.

"To know Dad better," Paolo continued.

Intrigued, she pulled back slightly from the embrace.

Amused by her reaction, he asked, "Shall I stay to learn more about a certain jaguar?"

Fabiana caressed his face with her fingertips adorned with a rosette pattern. She gazed into Paolo's magnetic eyes, which morphed into the eyes of the jaguar. Feeling the tingling sensation of excitement flowing through her, she whispered into his ears, "Let's find out by playing 'Who's the jaguar? Who's the prey'"

They purred playfully like a jaguar then locked themselves in a mutual gaze that felt like an eternity. A magnetic pull connected them, leading to an intense kiss that spoke volumes without words.

The End

ACKNOWLEDGMENTS

I am grateful to my two remarkable and fun Genes – Gene and Eugene. Thanks also to my wonderful Sally, as well as my supportive mother, sisters, family, and friends who stand by me and provide encouragement. My posthumous appreciation to my father, Zelinho, who loved the Pantanal and whose enduring wisdom remains a constant source of inspiration for me.

Thank you to Esteban Alvarado and the talented writers at the Writers Workshop in San Diego. Your insightful critiques, thoughtful feedback, and camaraderie have been instrumental in refining and elevating my manuscript.

My profound appreciation to Valerie Hansen, a prolific writer whose enthusiasm for the written word is truly inspiring. Your discerning editorial insights and dedication to nurturing literary voices have elevated my work to its utmost potential.

My heartfelt thanks to Anahita Ayasoufi, an accomplished writer who, amidst the pandemic, generously devoted time to connect with me via Zoom for shared writing sessions. Your kindness and the creation of a supportive community during those challenging times are truly valued.

A warm acknowledgment to Susan Lowe, Sue and Kayla McConchie, Dolores Smith, and Cynthia Q. Villanueva. Your readership has been a motivating factor, and I appreciate your insightful input and the valuable feedback and comments you've shared.

My special thanks to Joe, Amy, Frank and the editorial team for your expertise, guidance and the cover design that beautifully captures the essence of my book. Your dedication to achieving excellence has not only facilitated this journey but also made it more fulfilling.

I extend my appreciation to all those who have contributed to this literary journey, be it through encouragement, feedback, or shared moments. Your involvement has left a lasting impact on this book.

And to you, dear reader, I express my sincere thanks for taking the time to read this book – your support is truly valued.

***

May this fictitious story invite us to cherish our natural resources and the incredible wildlife.

***

Had fun reading?

Explore more with the following thought-provoking questions for a more engaging experience.

1. How do the jaguar's eyes serve as a metaphorical bridge between Fabiana's urban background and the untamed Pantanal, shaping her journey and sense of belonging?

2. In what ways do the characters Paolo and Glorieta embody the intensity and complexities of the jaguar's gaze, and how does their presence influence Fabiana's decisions and experiences?

3. As Fabiana reluctantly moves from Rio de Janeiro to the Pantanal, what challenges and discoveries await her in this untamed landscape, and how do they contribute to her character development?

4. The radio show "Words into Tangible Worlds" plays a significant role in unfolding Fabiana's story. How does Mrs. Mae's narrative style enhance the overall atmosphere and engagement of the tale?

5. With the untamed Pantanal as a backdrop, what mysteries and secrets might Fabiana uncover, and how do they contribute to the overall intrigue and captivation of the narrative?

What do you think?